Wakefield Press

SNOW

Gina Inverarity grew up in South Australia and worked for many years as an editor for a range of publishers. Her first children's book, *The Brown Dog*, was published in 2017.

Gina owns a forest in New Zealand and hopes to live in it one day. For now she lives in Wellington with her partner and two daughters. *Snow* is her first young adult novel.

SNOW

GINA INVERARITY

Wakefield
Press

Wakefield Press
16 Rose Street
Mile End
South Australia 5031
www.wakefieldpress.com.au

First published 2020

Cover designed by Liz Nicholson, Wakefield Press
Edited by Margot Lloyd, Wakefield Press
Typeset by Michael Deves, Wakefield Press
Printed in Australia by Ovato Book Printing,
formerly Griffin Press, Adelaide

ISBN 978 1 74305 700 1

NATIONAL LIBRARY OF AUSTRALIA

A catalogue record for this
book is available from the
National Library of Australia

CORIOLE
McLAREN VALE

Wakefield Press thanks
Coriole Vineyards for
continued support

For Ben

The clouding over

>>----->

The story of my birth is one I heard told. Even though I were there, without my own memory to call on I have to rely on the telling of others.

When I came into the world I brought a deep, soft quiet with me. For that is how the world is when it's covered in snow. Quiet. Like all the natural noises of people and creatures is muffled and smothered. The way the story goes is I arrived on a black night as cold as the frozen wastes to the south and, not long after, my mother fell ill with a burning fever, leaving her dead within days. So I was raised on the milk of whatever beast were available, there being no other nursing mothers in the chateau just then. As it were told to me, I drank from the teats of sheep and goats and even once a horse. I grew small and slow but I grew. With my mother gone and my father in a fog of grief, I kept to the kitchen and the yards where I were shown ways by whoever was about.

And all the while the seasons turned fierce and lengthened.

I remember riding my pony through the snowy forest near the chateau with my father. It wasn't always that we rode horses. There used to be vehicles and engines but they don't run on grass like horses can. And when the cold fell around here, in other parts there were storms and floods and fires and worse, and then there was no more fuel for vehicles and we went back to the old ways. Lucky for us, horses held no grudge against people for being turned out and overlooked those years when we liked our metal machines more, and they took bits in their mouths and saddles on their backs and returned to work for us like they had for centuries afore.

We were mushrooming that day, some still to be found where the branches grow so thick overhead the snow hadn't yet frozen the ground. I were up on my pony I named Gray, her harness painted with flowers. She followed the lead of my father's big bay, the fall of their feet muffled by the forest floor. I wish I knew then to drink in the warmer air and swallow the whole sky. Because you cannot put those things by for leaner times like you can a sack of potatoes. There were mushrooms plenty though and we picked a bundle.

'Don't pick those that show colour,' my father told me, 'for they are likely to make you sick.'

It were a shame, I thought, because the ones with colour were the pretty ones. Red caps with white spots, and bright orange bulges growing on the trunks of trees. But I were only allowed to touch the plain brown and white ones. Some were cooked for dinner and the rest were dried on racks, stalks withering and caps shrivelling slowly.

'Good for flavouren soups and stews,' Cook told me. She puffed them up with boiled water and it was like they were fresh-picked once again.

Cook's kitchen were set at the back of the main building opening onto the big yard. It were a long room with a table

2

set in the middle. At one end sat a big iron stove heated with a fire that burned day and night. Cook were old enough to remember electric kettles and grills and pans and it were one of her favourite things to groan about the loss of them. Being born into this way of living, electrics were just stories to me. And I loved that iron stove. In my mind it sat like a tired old dragon, belching smoke crossly if it weren't fed the right fuel at the right time, or sleeping contented when it had a good steady heat burning in its belly.

When my father were alive and there were still vegetables being grown and animals supplying milk and cheese and meat, Cook's kitchen were full of smells and wonders of edible creation. Stewed fruits and puddings and roasts and cheeses and cakes covered the table and there were always a bustle going on. Cook shouted orders and a couple of girls and a boy or two rushed to her bidding. There were a sink set out on the porch where a boy spent his days bent over washing the piles of dirty pans and plates that never ceased their coming. The kitchen were also safe from my stepmother, who never went there. And everyone living in the chateau passed through at one time or another, so it were the best place to sit quiet and hear some news.

When I were a baby I played under the great table. I were shooed away there when I got under Cook's feet. And when I was older, after my father died, it was a comfort to sneak in under there. I'd made myself a cosy spot one day when some strangers entered the kitchen, a mother and her children, looking for work. They'd come up from the lowlands, near the city, moving away from trouble there. The woman were vague on what exactly the upset had been.

Her husband weren't around, she said shortly. 'Gone from us,' were her answer to Cook's enquiry.

'Well,' Cook said, 'there int much work except what we do to survive another season. Everyone has to do something. What are your skills?'

'I'm a weaver by trade,' the woman replied. 'And my daughters all learning from me. If we have wool and flax we can make anything you need. And I see maybe you are. In need, that is.'

I heard a tired sigh come from Cook at her worn-out old towels and tablecloths being noticed by a stranger.

'I need an extra girl in the kitchen, if one of your daughters wants to learn,' she said. 'And even though all our cloths are worn out, there int anything but pride sayen we replace them afore they fall apart.'

'My boy can hunt,' the woman said, seeing now that as much as her skills were valued in the city, they might not be enough to save her up on the mountain. 'He learned from his father.'

From where I sat, not wanting to draw attention to my eavesdropping, I could only see a boy's legs stuck into boots too big for him, wearing trousers that looked to have been woven by his mother.

Cook were silent, considering. 'If you can squeeze in with another family and get along together without me hearing about it, you can stay. Have your samples ready and there's a chance Rain will like your work.' And, more to herself than anyone else, she said, 'Then you may wish you'd found another door to knock on.'

That all happened before I were locked away. I have passed three years now in a cold dark cell, plus nine afore that under the sky when my father lived still. So I have twelve years behind me and many more to live if I can escape. If I cannot leave my years are numbered. I'm not allowed a fire and the only way I'm not dead is the wall I share with my stepmother is well heated from the other side. Her fire burns night and day. If it even falls low she screams for it to be stoked back to glowing hot again. But though I follow the weak light as it travels across the floor of my room, exposing my cold skin to it, I know I can't survive shut away forever. Already I'm small for my age. One of the girls who brings me meals was a child the same as me, and while she grew over the years, I have not keep match with her. The thickest part of me is my black hair, braided like a rope.

There's a deep quiet in the chateau outside my high window. Another heavy snowfall in the long night and all sounds are muffled. The roof beams were groaning and creaking under the weight of it, until the men climbed up and pushed the snowfall off into the courtyards below. At any time I expected one of them to come crashing through and land in my room with me, the roof being in none too good a repair after many years of my stepmother's neglect.

After passing the dim hours of daylight in much the way I pass all others, by doing my wondering and singing softly to myself for company, I fell asleep when it were dark outside and in, there being no way to occupy myself when I can't see for blackness. I woke to the sound of riders coming in. I could hear the horses snorting, tryen to clear icicles from their nostrils. Apart from the clink of metal shoes on paving, I could not hear what was said by those who went out to greet them, nor see anything but the glow of torches against the stone walls of the yard. After some time I heard footsteps in the hall outside my room, heavy ones like those of men in riding boots.

I pressed my ear to the wall that I shared with my stepmother but could hear nothing but murmurs. It seemed the men were asken my stepmother questions, for they did most of the speaking. Then there were pauses before my stepmother's voice came back with short responses. It were a brief meeting and I were none the wiser as to the reason for their visit when the same boot steps passed by in the hallway again. The horses had been led to the stables, so the riders must have begged a bed for the rest of the long night.

There were no point lying awake looking at the blackness in front of my eyes. Best to close them and look at the dreams and memories that appeared like magic behind.

When the girl brought my bowl the next day she was in and out through the door like she couldn't move fast enough. And when the lock clicked after her I found something she'd left.

A knife.

And not one for spreading butter, but a sharp one for slitting throats, with a bone handle. I only let myself have a few seconds to admire it before I slipped it into my belt and pulled my ragged jumper low. Then I ate my food and curled up. It were bone-chilling cold, and there being nothing to do to pass the day but huddle close to the wall, I did so, keeping my blankets wrapped tight around me. There was something afoot and I wanted to be ready to face it so I tried to stay awake but my full belly had its own opinion and I must have fallen asleep.

I awoke to the sound of my door swinging open. As I sat up on my cot, a spirit lantern dazzled me, and I realised I'd slept through the short day and it was now night.

'Get up and come with me.'

Shielding my eyes to adjust them as quick as I could, I saw a man in the doorway. He wore leathers and boots, and the fur wrapped around his shoulders looked like dog. A firearm hung across his back so I took him for a hunter. He held the lantern in one hand and a hatchet like you use to chop kindling for a fire in the other. There were a threat in that tool, even though he did not wave it at me. Instead it hung in a loose grip at his side. Still, I weren't arguing with a lump of sharp steel, so I followed.

The hall outside my room was cold and I shivered from it, crossing my arms over my chest.

'Get your coat,' he told me.

I looked at him, still confused by being woken from my sleep.

'You have no coat?' the hunter said.

'No,' I replied, and before thinking I added, 'What would I have need of a coat for when I've been shut away these long years?'

I only received a grunt in reply and no swinging of the hatchet for my boldness so I asked, 'Where am I going?'

Seeing that this caused the hunter's fingers to curl tightly around the handle of the hatchet, I paid mind and shut my mouth.

We passed through the chateau in the darkest of the night. For certain no one saw us for they lay aslumber under all the piles of warmth they could find, only sending out an arm from time to time to sling another brick to the fire. If the hearth heat dies then that may be the beginning of a much longer sleep than intended.

The snow crunched softly under my feet and it did not once occur to me to cry out or protest because all I could do was look up in awe at the night sky. Though it were dense with dark cloud cover, it was nevertheless the first time I'd been outside under it in too long and I craned my neck to feel the expanse above me. Until I tripped and fell to my hands and knees.

The hunter grabbed me under my arm and hauled me back on my feet hissing, 'Watch yourself,' not unkind, but I left the sky to its business after that and looked to where I stepped.

Once through the gates, which had been left ajar, we stayed close to the outer wall, moving to the west. It seemed to me the hunter were unwilling to break out onto the open ground, even with the moon long hidden away these years and the thick sky to cover us. We paused while he doused the lantern and when that dim glow faded I could barely see my own hand in front of my face. We stayed put while our eyes grew accustomed and when I could make out the hunter as a darker blur in my side vision, he set off once again. Then I felt my way along with my feet and my ears, my eyes being of little use. We sank to our knees in the snow but by listening careful liken I found I could put my feet in his footsteps and save the trouble of breaking my own trail. Still, the hunter's stride was twice my own so every step was a stretch.

It were not long afore my toes were numb and my teeth chattering together making a racket that might have woken the chateau, even at a distance. I did not complain. Whatever were in front of me was better than what were behind for the simple fact of it being outside and not shut up behind a bolted door. I had been cold for three years and I dared to think I could get a lot colder before my lights blinked out.

The hunter halted.

It were still too dark to see much of anything but I felt him come close and loom over me as a darker blur. I flinched and my hand went to the handle of my new knife. But then I smelt his smell, which put me in mind of my father. I told myself quick that if I had to I would stick the shiny metal into the hunter's belly for the chance of a head start. Trouble with that plan were having no idea as to where I was or where to head for. I wouldn't live until morning if I were on my own.

And while my mind flicked around my skull like a panicked mouse, instead of killing me the hunter slung a fur around my shoulders. It were light as air and warm as a den of dogs. He said nothing and turned back to his trail-breaking. I had to follow quick so I kept my quiet but I thought, he hasn't kild me yet. And why keep me warm if he plans to?

The rest of the long night even those two thoughts fell silent as all I could do was lift one foot and put it in front of the other. I'd been long idle in my cell and my legs were not used to walking. It seemed to me that the hunter's strides became shorter for it weren't as much of a reach for his next step. And then suddenly, like the light were playing a little one's game of jumping out from behind corners to scare people, I found I could use my eyes again. The sky above had turned from dense and dark to glowing and grey and there were nothing to see ahead but forest, not more'n a few hundred paces away.

'Hurry,' said the hunter and lengthened his stride.

It weren't in my power to do any hurrying, steel hatchet or none. My feet were frozen blocks and my knees had lost their bend. The dog fur was keeping the warmth in my chest and belly but my hands may as well have been detached and left behind in the snow for all I could feel them. As the hunter drew away from me, I had to stop. It weren't that I didn't want to follow. I had no thoughts of escape; I had no thoughts at all. Just cold all the way through to the marrow of my bones. And if that weren't all the shame I needed, I felt tears leaking out of my eyes and freezing where they fell on my cheeks. My nose ran while it could and then froze along with my tears.

When the hunter turned and ploughed back to me I expected him to cuff my ears and slap me to my senses. And for sure I would've preferred that, because instead he scooped me up and carried me like a baby all the way to the forest.

The hunter

The next thing I knew was the crackle of a fire and the smell of smoke. I was lying on the hunter's coat with the dog fur over me. My boots were drying and my feet wrapped in a woollen cloth. I couldn't remember when I'd last been so toasty warm, the more wondrous for being outside with nothing but fresh frozen air all around. Above me conifers groaned as if they were protesting the burden of snow they'd caught on their branches. At times the load became too great and a tree set loose a branch to save its life, the forest floor littered with fallen limbs. The crack and crash then was the only sound to break the deep hush.

I sat up, taking care not to let cold air under my cosy cave of fur, and looked for the hunter. I could see fresh tracks leading away from the fire but none returning. Too late and awful sorry for it, I felt for my knife and found it gone. I were disarmed.

I kicked off my woollen muff in a tantrum and pulled on my damp boots to stamp around the fire looking, as if I could have found my knife just fallen in the snow.

Don't be an idiot, you stupid girl, I said to myself. The knife is gone and now your chances of living another day are even less than they were afore in the tower room.

When I finished my stomping, I sat on the hunter's coat and put my head on my knees to think a moment. But it were hard to concentrate over the rumbling of my stomach and instead I took to staring into the wondrous fire crackling in its snowy bed. I held out my palms to feel the warmth. The hunter suddenly appeared back at the fireside without me even noticing his approach.

Pay some mind afore not paying any is the last thing you do, I told myself.

Wordlessly the hunter plucked the bright green feathers off a parrot he'd shot, pulled out its guts and flung them away, drew a stick through the carcass and set it to roasting over the coals. Try as I might I could not tear my eyes from that roasting meat. I stood to carefully turn it soas it became brown all over, like I'd seen done in Cook's kitchen. The hunter took back his coat and shrugged it on, slinging his firearm over one shoulder and keeping an eye on me.

We ate the bird with our fingers. I ate every morsel I could find and licked the grease from my fingers one by one, not giving a rat's eye about manners, which I probably should have seeing as it was the first meal I'd eaten in company in three years.

And once that bird hit my belly, my thoughts came alive again.

'Did you take my knife?' I asked the hunter as I wiped my hands on my pants.

'I did,' he replied.

'Why?'

'I'm not keen on haven you poke holes in me when I'm trying to catch a nap.'

'Why should I kill you? You've done me none but favours to now. And I'm glad to be out of that tower and away from her.'

The hunter did not answer and I could not read his face.

But I already knew the answer. It had been in the pit of my belly this whole time. Once the bird meat landed on top of it, it rose up and finally made its way to my mind.

The hunter stood and started kicking snow over the fire. It hissed and smoked in a sodden fury at being put out.

'What are you going to do to me?'

My fear overtook what little wisdom I had gained in my twelve years and I stood up with my fists clenched. 'Tell me, what are your orders, Hunter?'

'You're to be kild and your warm heart brought back to her as proof,' he said flatly, squatting near the smoking fire.

'Why now, when I been locked up all these years? I would have died from not seeing the sky before too much longer, then she could have laid me in the tomb beside my father and been done with it.'

'Seems she couldn't wait. Seems the matter became pressing.'

'Something to do with the riders that arrived a night ago?' I asked him.

The hunter looked into my face then. 'What do you know about that?'

'Nothen but muffled words I couldn't hear proper,' I conceded.

'My orders were to get you away fast and quiet. And bring her back something to show I'd done my work,' he finished, shaking his head and prodding the dying fire with the toe of his boot.

When I looked into his face then I saw a boy rather than the man he'd appeared to be in the dark of night. He were only a few years older than me, but grown proper having been outside in the fresh air eating roasted birds as he liked, and lengthening his legs with walking. My legs were like the rest of me, small from being shut up like a pet tortoise in a bowl. The hunter wore his hair shaved at the sides to show markings set under the skin that told he were a first-born son, his father dead but his mother living still. Three sisters came after him and the years in his trade showed as six arrow-shaped marks at his left temple. I could also see his life hadn't been all as he'd liked because a scar ran across his nose and under his eye and there were shadows beneath his cheekbones that showed he'd known worry. Which, given his present task, I took for true. Something about the weave of his trousers brought back a memory.

'Aren't you the boy come with his mother and sisters to the chateau kitchen, years ago, looking for work?'

The hunter looked up at me.

'I remember your boots were too big for you.'

'You were there?'

'I were hid under the table, keeping out of the way.'

'The boots belonged to my father afore me.'

'What happened to him soas he had no need of his boots anymore?'

The hunter looked away to the trees. 'He weren't a good man and all I can say is he maybe shouldn't have taught me so well which end of an axe works better than the other.'

Perhaps the killing of me weren't the first sorry task the hunter had turned his hand to afore this. The darkness in his face showed me both the good news that he dint take kindly to violence but also the bad news that he'd nevertheless done as he had to. As I understand it, it makes no difference to be kild by someone who doesn't have the heart for it as by someone who does. The end result is you're dead and the difference is none.

'Why give me your fur and feed me? Do you prefer to murder girls with warm blood and full bellies? Are you a monster as well as a hunter?'

I said this fiercely, and as soon as the words left my lips, I knew I'd misjudged. The hunter's face hardened and too late I perceived that I was making his killing easier if I called him names.

'Little Queen,' he sneered, 'I'm doing my job or else I'm dead. That's the way of the world now. Stamping your foot and given me orders makes no difference. I have mine from higher than you. The way I see it, it's your blood or mine. And as I hold all the steel, I'm placing my bets against little girls with none but high and haughty tempers.'

With this the hunter drew his hatchet from his belt and wrapped his fingers around the handle.

I may have lost my blade, but with roasted bird in my belly my wits were returning to me.

'Why do you call me Little Queen?'

The hunter lowered his chin to his chest. 'That's what they call you in the chateau,' he said. 'The tenants. They call you the Little Queen in the tower. And they wonder what it was you did to Rain to make her hate you as she does.'

The hunter frowned here, like he'd like to know it too.

I weren't going to satisfy his curiosity just so he could get to killen me sooner. Besides, all I'd done to make her hate me was be born.

'That knife were given to me by someone in the chateau who wants to open the odds against hunters with steel.'

He hesitated. 'It's true there are those whose sympathies lie more with you than with her. That being no surprise after the way she carries on, making life a misery. Still, she owns the dwellings and the land and there's few feel like going out on their own. They'd rather hide behind stout walls with safety in numbers than be out in the long nights on their own. Including me. So I'll be doing my job as paid for.'

'What does she pay you?' Asking him questions was keeping my warm heart beating on the right side of my chest and best it stayed that way as long as possible.

'That's none of your business, Little Queen. Unless you think you can match it?' the hunter said, smiling with one side of his face.

I considered my assets. My knife stolen, they were none but the clothes I stood up in and then even the fur borrowed.

'I'll claim my father's house when I'm of age.'

'It be your word against hers and she's in possession. No law or lawmakers to back your claim hereabouts.'

'I'll wed you when I'm grown,' I said, taking a gamble. Promises that are a long time coming can be overtaken by fate in the meanwhile. 'In exchange for my life.'

The hunter scoffed. 'Could be a while in the waiting,' he said. 'Not sure I got that kind of time being as how small you're starting out. But if you're offering, then I accept your proposal. I have no appetite for killen children today and she'll know no difference between your heart and a piglet's.'

Winning caught me unawares. If he never intended to kill me I'd given my betrothal away for free.

He slid his axe through his belt and turned to leave.

'Don't head back the way of the chateau if you value your beating heart or your future husband's, Little Queen,' he called over his shoulder. 'You can keep the dog fur as an engagement gift.'

I'd been furious all my life with Rain, but that was being bested by my fury at the hunter as he turned away from me, stepping into our tracks from the night afore. Outwitted by a hunter was hard for my pride to take. And while my thoughts chased each other around, going nowhere, he was leaving me.

'Hunter!' I yelled in a panic. 'You must leave me my knife or you are killen me anyway. But slow and of cold, and that is meaner than killen me fast and warm.'

The hunter paused. I saw his hand go to his belt as he turned back toward me and then all manner of events happened in one moment.

There was a rush of cold air behind me and I were pushed face-first to the snow, where I lay stunned. A great weight were on my back and I heard a snarling I took to be from a bear. A big one, judging by how I was pinned to the ground, my face smashed into the sharp top layer of snow. Then, just as I were wondering if I could draw my last breath before my ribs were crushed, or whether my throat would be torn out first, the hunter gave a shout and the bear turned. She stepped from my back and started running toward him, but clumsily, for the snow were deep and soft. I raised my head and saw the hunter swing his firearm from his back in one motion, bullet already in the chamber, and squeeze the trigger.

The bear dropped mid-stride, and her last breath left her body afore she fell in the snow.

I climbed to my hands and knees and retched as a surge of fright passed along my nerves. I had sense enough to keep my breakfast in my belly but only by an effort of breathing slow and long. I dug my fingers in the snow to feel the icy cold and bring me back to my senses. It took an effort but slowly the world stopped spinning and I sat back on my heels to take in the scene.

The danger was past but I were sorry to see that saving my life had cost that of a mother bear, for a cub wandered out of the forest and pushed up against the dead body. It were a wee thing, hardly to my knee and still showing all the sweet roundness of a baby.

'Are you hurt?' said the hunter to me, and I shook my head. 'Dammit, dammit,' he said. 'I wouldn't have kild her, if she hadn't been about to rip off your head, then mine.'

I knelt next to the mother bear and stroked her fur, sayen my sorries, and not ashamed to let the hunter see that I shed tears for such a beautiful creature in spite of her menace. She were only trying to protect her cub, though she were worried for nothing. We must have been camping on her trail and coming across us gave her as much of a scare as she'd given me.

There never used to be such an animal as a bear on these islands but when the cities flooded, all manner of beasts that had been shut in cages for people's amusement were set free. Not all of them lived, being unsuited for life in this new and different wilderness, but the bears found the land to their liking and prospered, even though they were the first of their kind to walk here.

Like a wild dog's, a bear's fur were valued for warmth and not to be left rotting in the snow. And so now the hunter, pushing the cub and me to the side, made quick work of removing that mother bear's skin. It were too much gore for me to watch and I crossed the clearing, keeping my back to the hunter's sorry work, and set about reviving the fire he'd kicked over. It gave my fingers something to do and a task for my mind as I recovered my senses from the scare. After a time the hunter bundled up the fur, tying it with leather straps, to be cured by the tanners at the chateau, and took one last thing from the bear as he stood. I saw then that he held the mother bear's heart, dripping on the bloody mess of snow around what were left of her.

'I have my proof now,' he said. 'You can thank the she-bear for that. You're free to go, Little Queen. Head west. Look for a camp of miners. I know of no women stopping there but perhaps they will take you in if you offer to work for them. And you may have your blade back.'

With this, the hunter stuck my knife in the snow where he stood and took his leave, bear blood marking his trail.

Snow alone

My father named me for the freshly fallen snow. At the beginning of the clouding over it were just a name, but later it came to feel like a curse, a constant reminder of hardship. The long nights season draws longer every year and when the ground is frosty, there can be no crops planted or harvested. With the rivers and lakes frozen, even drawing water is a chore that takes a whole day. People pray for the sun to once again burn through the thick layers of cumulus between the earth and the heavens but all for nothing. There are no prayers strong enough to lift the sky. They are wasting precious energy they could be using to draw another breath.

I waste no air on prayers. They have done me no good so far.

It were a long cold night that followed after the hunter left. The twilight lingered under the heavily laden boughs of the forest trees. The dying of the day like a trickster, fading slowly and then surprising me by suddenly turning black. I nursed my fire into life and collected damp wood. It burnt, but low.

I'd never heard a bear cub cry before and it broke my heart to hear it now. That cub kneaded what was left of the she-bear but got no comfort as the cold air drew out what was left of her warmth. I wished the cub would come and join me at my fire.

I'd have welcomed the company of even a sharp-toothed wild creature such as she as I shivered in my bed of snow. I felt my thoughts slow to a honey-like consistency and a golden liquidy warmth spread through my blood. My eyelids were heavy and it would have been the very peak of pleasure to let them close. But a part of my brain, deep down in the back, sent out a jolt. If I slept then it would be the last thing I did. I were freezing my way to dying and there were only one way to save myself.

I took my knife and crept over to the she-bear carcass, placing a hand on the crying cub, for my own comfort as much as hers. The hunter had left the head and scruff, perhaps as no mistake, because now I took my knife and cut away the fur. When I were done I placed the she-bear's skull over my own, which fit like a crown forged special for me, and wrapped her scruff around my shoulders. It were still a slimy mess but it brought me up warm in a moment. I crept back to my snow bed by the low fire and passed into dreams of climbing inside the bodies of slain creatures and wrapping myself in their slippery innards. Before the light of the next day came I were aware of the cub, finally come to curl up with me, and with her blessing the visions passed away and we fell into a dreamless slumber.

I woke to the bear baby kneading my front and nuzzling under my furs.

'There's none there of what you're looking for,' I told her, sitting up and pushing her away. 'It's a hard day's wean you've got ahead of you, you silly wee thing.'

The cub sat on her haunches and looked at me scornful liken.

'Sorry to be the bearer of woeful news but the sooner you get used to it, the better for us both,' I told her.

There were nothing to be had for my breakfast either. Even the bones of the parrot had been buried by a fresh fall of snow. I brushed the frost off as I stood and stamped my feet to warm them. Now that I had a wealth of two furs, I fashioned myself a skirt from the dog fur by tying it about my waist over my long pants. Then, settling the she-bear head and scruff as comfortable on my head and shoulders as were possible, I looked to the way the hunter had pointed and set off in that direction, sinking ankle-deep in the snow.

It were a day no one remembers when the sun disappeared. A span of a day or two of overcast skies and no one thought anything of it. And then the grey piled up and it were grey upon grey. After a month people were shaking their heads in wonder. Where was the sun?

It were called the clouding over after that. And even now, there are some who look up from their work from time to time, willing the white to part for a glimpse of sunshine. My father told me he'd looked up into clear blue sky over and over without thinking a thing about it but when it was gone he wished he could have every one of those times back to keep them lasting longer.

It were a cold morning to start a march on an empty stomach, and as far as I could tell from her crying, the bear cub was in agreement. As was a habit in my cell I passed the hours walking by letting memories come back to me.

After my mother died, Rain came along. She convinced my father to marry her in secret and made the announcement to me along with the rest of the chateau, like I weren't even family, let alone my father's first-and-only daughter. I heard the kitchen girls say that she'd left her own children along with their father. Always looking for greener fields, she were. When she first came she looked on me and weren't approving of what she saw. I'd been allowed to turn feral, she told my father. He had no ideas about how to raise a girl, she told him. My pony was turned out and instead I were made to wear dresses and sit while my hair was fussed with and I were prodded and poked and plucked until she was satisfied.

My father had swelled up in his joints by then and every movement were painful for him. He couldn't think how to make a life without my mother so he let himself be told how to be by Rain. As the long nights settled in, it made his pain worse and his new wife soothed him with her honey voice, nothing being too much trouble if it brought him comfort. She doted on him, caring for every need he may or mayn't even known he had. She ordered him broths and sat with him while he sipped at them, whispering and laughing softly.

At such times I saw them I dint doubt she loved him. He were the only person she was kind toward, and it weren't just for his house and possessions. But while my father went on getting more and more feeble, she crept in and spread herself about. After she had me smoothed over she set her sights on the chateau, throwing out the tenants she didn't like the look of and letting stay those who were quick to scramble to her word. She added gilt and glamour to the main house that were not to my liking and she told the tenants what to do as if the words were coming from my father. She told them to grow food. She told them to make heat and power for her or their children would freeze when she cast them out of their homes.

After a while she forbade me visiting my father in case I did something to make things worse, though what that may have been by sitting by his bed and spenden time, I never knew. But she were like a child with elbows spread wide to keep all the cakes to herself, shutting me out and keeping my father's company for herself. I should have done more but instead I spent as much time out of her sight as I could, in the kitchen with Cook and in the yards, though I weren't allowed to ride my pony anymore. Instead I did all the feeding of the animals pushed aside by their mothers. There were always goats and lambs crying and it were tedious work to give them the bottle. The hands in charge were of the mind that letting them die were more natural. If the mothers had rejected them, maybe there were a good reason for it, just not one plain enough to see. I weren't in agreement and took it on myself to gather and feed them all through the day and night. If I came under Rain's eye after doing it, covered with grit and wearing working clothes, I were subject to her wrath. She couldn't stand it. I'd be made to sit through more bathing and plucking and poking and straightening and primping and preening and posing.

She had her people recording everything in pictures. She told me people in the city where she came from liked to see how people like us lived. I couldn't see the sense in that because how she carried on weren't how we lived at all. Outside the chateau people were labouring over growing food and tending animals and clearing snow from spouts and roofs so they dint collapse on our heads. What she was doing had nothing to do with getting prepared to survive through another season of long nights.

It were the last time she made me sit for one of her family portraits, when I were getting a little older, primped and preened and kicking my heels with a scowl on my face, that she finally cracked. The scene were all faked for the picture. She had people dressed up in costumes, a Cook, a Hunter, a Milkmaid, a Groom, her idea of mountain folk. Rain stood at the front, swathed in silks and feathers such as no sane mountain person wore for the sensible reason they'd soon lose their fingers and toes from frostbite. No one there were the real people doing that work, them being too busy actually doing those jobs to spare time for dressing up.

The photographer, travelled up from the city, suggested I be put more in the front, that people were asking to see more of the girl, dark of hair and eye, and with the cross face. Who is she? What's her story? He said they wanted to know.

My stepmother was furious with me for stealing the attention away from her. Even though I had no interest in doing so. I were only there because she had someone drag me out from under Cook's table. It led to angry words for it were the false accusation that I could not bear. I wanted no part in her performance, and I were doing nothing but what I were told. To be accused of having too much pride and attention-stealing was more than I could take.

She pulled me by the arm out to the hallway and yelled at me there.

'You're a selfish wee brat and nothing but trouble!' she told me. 'I try my best to give you a chance of a better future but you'll never come to nothing.'

'You int my mother, so it's none of your concern what happens to me,' I answered back coldly.

'You're a dirty little stray and I don't know why my husband ever loved you,' Rain told me, hands on her hips and swaying over me in a fury.

I pushed her. I were only ten years old but on her teetering high heels she were easily overbalanced and when she fell it were backward down the stairs.

She tumbled all the way to the bottom, flinging out her arms to catch herself and then screeching when they bent back underneath her the wrong way. She only stopped when she hit the bottom stair and then were deathly still.

I've kild her, I thought, with my child's mind.

And then her people rushed down to her and I saw she weren't dead at all, just hurt a bit but making it seem worse than it were by crying and putting on a trembling in the finger she pointed at me.

I was struck all over with horror. What were I thinking trying to kill a person? That weren't how I'd been taught by my gentle father. I covered my mouth with my hands and said I was sorry over and over. But her pride was dangerous damaged and my sorries were not accepted.

Soon after that I were locked in the tower room.

I weren't a hunter, even now I had my knife back. Mushrooming was my only skill but I didn't fancy the eating of any fungus I saw growing on the trunks of the trees we passed. I sucked on snow when I became thirsty but the body gets dryer in the cold than you'd think and my mouth was parched as a stone. The bear cub stopped to lick the bark of trees so I followed her lead and found some relief in the moisture to be had there. At what I judged to be midday, I sat in the snow to rest. The cub climbed into my lap and curled up for a nap. Tame as a housecat she were already, though she took me for her mother, and I were just a poor milkless substitute. The warm honey of sleep started beckoning me afore long so I forced myself up and to keep on the move.

We followed deer trails in the main, the forest being too dense to forge our own path. The deer were in no hurry was the problem, and they wandered from one clearing to another in no particular direction. I could see where they'd been scratching the snow away to graze on what little grass they could find there. We came upon none of the animals as we travelled, for they smelled the she-bear and were out of our way quick.

As we trudged over the snow, the forest darkened, and it weren't just the sun sinking in the sky after its short work of the day. The trees grew closer together and there were more of the giant cold-bearing types with thin needley leaves that whisper together in the high branches. It's a known fact that trees have more to say to each other than people are smart enough to realise. They talk together with their roots, sending chemical signals and passing them along through the closely woven web of forest.

I had the feeling that our arrival was expected long before we passed under the branches, and now all that was left were gossipy chatter about my business. I tried to ignore them. If they were to be no help, it just seemed mean to talk about me out of my hearing. The little bear seemed spooked, like as me, and stuck to my heels.

But then our luck turned, or perhaps the trees were not as set against us as I'd taken them to be, for we came across a branch, cracked but not fallen away from its trunk, forming a shelter covered with snow. I crawled in head first and found a cosy cave there. For sure, it were another bed of ice, but with my furs and the little bear it soon warmed up enough to sleep once again. This time my dreams were of food, and not the bowls of nothing much that I'd been fed all those years in the tower room, but instead all the meals I'd had before that. I dreamed of Cook's spiced buns and rabbit stew and crisp potatoes and roasted birds and smoked fish traded with those from down the valleys where lakes and rivers were not frozen over. And mushrooms and cheese and cream and milk. My stomach ate itself through the night and when we woke early the next morning I had cramps from hunger.

I'll be doing Rain's own dirty murdering job if I die of starving out here, I told myself. All my body wanted was stay in our cosy cave the rest of the day and forever, but I forced myself to dig out the overnight snowfall and crawl out into the morning. The little bear were even more sad and slow than I and poked out her nose and none else. I staggered a few steps and turned back.

'Come on, Little Bear,' I called. 'We can make it. This day will bring a meal for me and milk for you, but not by hiding away. At least we're under the sky and finding a life to live.' And with that, she scrambled to her feet and padded unsteadily after me.

It were clear the deer trails were leading downhill. I kept my back to the weak light filtering through the cloud cover as much as I could soas to be headed west in the direction the hunter had told me. There were nothing else to be done except place one foot in front of the other and keep it up. I dared not stop at all for fear I'd never get going again and my mind went as blank as a frozen lake.

Not even the wild dogs that I could hear from time to time,

getting braver and moving closer, stirred alarm. They barked out short calls to each other now and then, shadowing us off to the side and keepen downwind. No doubt they were puzzling out the strange mixture of bear carcass, live bear, and human girl scents and thinking it best to keep a distance to be on the safe side. Dogs are smart though and it wouldn't be long before they took a risk to come closer and then they'd figure out I was fooling them. The bear cub and I needed to cover some ground.

Little Bear stuck to me like my shadow, having her own animal senses for danger. The dogs were closing in, figuring out, slow liken but certain, that this odd party of girl and bear were going to be their next meal. And so, with my brain so hungry and frozen, it took me a while to see that we'd left the forest and even more surprising was the snow had thinned and we were crossing over tussock country. No doubting the ground was still frozen, but it was this country the deer came to for their grazing for the most part and then they took cover from dogs in the forest the rest of the time.

My eyes were not used to seeing colours that weren't white or whiteness, or grey or greyness, so the tawny golds and brown-greens of tussock country shot some alertness into my blood. And it were just as well because the dogs could clearly see now that I walked on two legs, and they had broken from their loping into trotting, rounding us up from the rear and no doubt driving us into the jaws of their packmates waiting out in front.

I broke into a run downhill, the hillside becoming steeper.

'Come on, Little Bear,' I urged the cub as she scrambled to keep up with me over the uneven ground.

If I wanted to avoid the dogs' trap I had to outsmart them, because there was no way my two legs were outrunning their four. So I took a sharp turn and headed along the contour of the hillside instead of making my way straight down which were the way my tired legs were telling me to go, and the way the dogs were pressing us along to.

Headed this way brought us onto the path of a young dog, gold of coat, with a bull-shaped head and lips lifted in a snarl, now standing his ground and me and Little Bear pounding toward him. His weight shifted to his hind legs as we came closer and I read inexperience in the whites of his eyes. The pack had put him out on the flank to watch and learn, and now he weren't sure what to do.

I put my head down and bent into a crouch as I ran, bringing the she-bear's head and snout down in a fearsome display of charging bear and, just to be sure, I started up shouting and roaring as I ran toward the gold dog.

It were too much confusion for him and he retreated. This broke the line and Little Bear and I raced through. We had a start and it would take the pack a minute to sort themselves back into the hunt. It weren't much of an advantage but we weren't dog food yet.

Little Bear was slowing, and too heavy for me to pick up and carry. So instead of leaping over tussocks in panic, I picked us a path around them and she kept up better. Glances to the side told me the dogs were forming up around us again. Those left behind had run hard to catch up. The harder the run, the more desperate it made them. But those dogs weren't the only ones desperate on that hillside. Me and Little Bear were two nights in the cold with empty bellies and this run was our last before we dropped dead in our tracks, so we knew to give it all we had.

My breath was ragged and burning in my throat, my chest heaving, and legs, which weren't strong to start with, turning to jelly.

And then I spied it, in a valley beneath us: a row of cabins set against a steep rocky wall, deep in shadow. I had to pick our descent on the run, as there weren't time to stop and find a line, so we ended up slipping down a field of open scree the last part, Little Bear on her front in a long skid, me on my backside, hands and elbows getting cut up as I tried to control my slide. We hit the bottom and rolled to a stop. Looking up, the dogs had halted at the edge, looking to their she-dog leader for orders. She backed away and turned to circle around. She were wise enough not to risk the soft pads of paws on sharp slate.

I ran to the closest cabin and turned the handle. Bolted. Three more I tried before I found one mercifully left unlatched and Little Bear and I fell inside and slammed the door after us. I leaned my back against that solid lump of wood and never more grateful to a door and four walls would I ever be. Little Bear lay on her side, panting and frothing at the mouth. I could see her ribs rising and falling even through her thick fur. The babe were not yet weaned and were far from done with her mother's milk for fattening up. Two days without that rich food plus some hard running and she were down to her last reserves.

I set aside my she-bear scruff, hauled myself to my feet for the cub's sake more'n mine and started to rummage through the cabin for food. I'd seen no livestock near the settlement so I had little hope of finding any fresh cow or goat milk, and there were nothing but maps and tools stored in the cupboards. I cursed myself for being in such a panic to get in. I shoulda looked for the mess hut. There weren't any point finding shelter and then still starving to death with dogs howling at the door.

The last cupboard I wrenched open though were a stash of emergency supplies: a bottle of water, dried venison, milk powder and hard oat biscuit. I mixed up the milk first and fed it to Little Bear off a spoon, whispering to her that it were good food and she had to eat, but then she got a taste for it and lapped it up straight from a bowl. I saved a bit for myself and gave the cub a strip of dried meat. She held it between her front paws all endearing and gnawed on it with her sharp baby teeth. The oat biscuit had to be soaked before I could chew on it and the rest of the water I drank in long gulps, forgetting to leave some for later. I ate half of that hard oat biscuit and then my belly said enough for now. Little Bear curled into my front like she'd taken to doing and we fell deep and heavy into sleep.

Dogs prowling outside and scratching at the door or not, we were done.

The miners

>>————————>

When the miners came back from their long day underground, they were startled to find a girl and a bear asleep in their hut.

Black from head to toe with the filth of the mine where they dug for crumbs of coal that fed the fires that made power for those who could afford it in the city, they were men nuggety of build and rough of tongue. When they poked us awake with their dirty boots, Little Bear whimpered and hid away beneath my furs. I wrapped my arms around her and told them sorry for breaking in and apologies for raiding their supplies but we'd been hunted down by dogs and it were desperation pure and simple that drove us through their door.

'Where're you from, girl?'

I were vague. 'Up the mountain above the snowline,' I said.

From the hard looks of them, the men carried stories of their own they'd rather not be telling and so had some respect for me keeping mine to myself. Little Bear were explained by the bloody she-bear fur I wore but I led them to believe I'd come across her mother already dead. From lack of food, perhaps, I suggested.

'There's so much blasting game for a bear up that mountain she'd only need to stick out a paw to pin down a bunny,' one of them scoffed.

I said nothing in reply.

'She's got a look of Voyager about her, you ask me,' said one who puffed on a pipe hanging from the corner of his mouth.

'Could be she's from those folks that wander over from time to time,' another agreed.

They all considered this as I frowned at them for referring to me as if I weren't a person sitting right there in front of them.

'Camp is no place for a girl,' said the one who I took for the boss.

'We got nowhere else to go,' I said, feeling desperation creeping up. 'Those dogs out there got a nose for us now. Pushing us out will be murdering us both. We won't take up space.'

'We all work for our living here,' said the boss. 'There's none to spare for guests.'

'I'll work in the mine with you,' I said. 'I'm stronger than I look.'

They all laughed, which were plain rude.

'Seeing as you look weak as water, even accounting for your hidden strength, it won't be any use at the work we do,' the boss said.

'I'll cook for you then,' I said reluctantly. 'And clean.'

They looked at me doubtful liken.

After some more pleading I weren't proud of, they agreed I could stay awhile.

My offer were brazen since I'd never cooked a meal or

washed a dish in my short life. With twelve men in the camp, though, I had plenty of chances to do my work poorly until I had it figured out.

It was rough toil mining the mountain with nothing but hands and picks. The days of big engines and blasting chemicals were behind us, and like all the other trades, the miners were back to the old ways. This made the work hard and the men harder. I found them crude of habit and humour, short of both stature and conversation, their words mostly coming in grunts and outbursts of barking laughter that I could never see the funny side of, and with rare a kind word. I learned quick to keep Little Bear out of their way, for they were likely to give her a boot in the ribs if they felt her teeth coming too close to their ankles.

So I found myself in a trap of a different kind. One made of effort from dawn to dark. The only good part was the men left camp early and returned late, leaving me alone for the daylight hours, short though they were. I taught myself to cook by making a mess and learning from it each time. I served the food and filled their cups with the rank beer they brewed themselves from pine needles.

I had a hut to share with my bear. It were dank and dark but no more so than the tower room I'd left behind. And this one had a door I could open as I pleased. I swept the floor and made myself a hard bed from a pallet and tussock grass. I were allowed to take the wax from the table when the candles were none but stubs and melt them together for a light at the end of my working day. With just this flickering flame to see by, and my cub for company, my hut after a while felt something like home. My mind turned to old habits, following thoughts down memory holes that wound around and around, leading me further and further along dark tunnels.

One morning long ago before I were locked away I crept into my father's sick room during the weak light of morning. He were on the top floor, down the end of a long hall. To get there I had to sneak past Rain's sitting room. She kept the door ajar at all times, to watch for people trying to pay visits on my father. This day though, I waited patient liken at the top of the stairs, standing in socks. When I heard Rain begin to rummage about her things, talking to herself softly as was her habit, I hurried past, avoiding all the creaky spots on the old floor. When I slipped in the door I went to my father's bedside.

'I'm poorly today, my love,' he said, coughing. 'With a thick head and wet lungs.' He patted my hand. 'Run away and feed your lambs.'

I dint do as he said right away, having taken so much trouble to get there.

After a time he stirred again and now he seemed different, full of intent. 'Snow, my sweet girl, listen to me now. When I am gone, the mountain is left to you.'

I shook my head and held his hand, not wanting to hear such talk.

'Your stepmother will keep it in trust for you until you come of age. I have her word and there be no need to put it in writing among those dearest to me.'

I nodded, tears falling on my cheeks.

'Now, now, none of that,' he said and I did my best to stop crying, not wanting him to see me sad. When I'd wiped my eyes he were soporous, his breath raspy.

I sat with him quietly then, my gaze wandering the room and my thoughts sliding away, leaving just a feeling like I'd lost something. It felt like something more important than a glove or a pet rock, so why couldn't I think what it was?

Later that day, my father passed away with no one near.

I weren't allowed to see him again, or attend his burial. But there were a place I knew where I could climb up a ladder left careless, and from there step across to the top of the chateau wall, and it was from there that I watched. I saw Rain follow the men carrying his body, wrapped in a shroud, through the snow. More men walked beside, carrying all the firearms available to ward off the wild animals that Rain had an unnatural fear of. No dog were brave or stupid enough to attack a large group of people in the middle of the day, even I knew, but she never left the chateau's walls without a guard.

The ground were too frozen to bury a body, and fuel too precious for burning one, so there was a tomb down the way, a snow cave blocked with stone blocks, where all the dead bodies were sealed away. The wall had been disassembled and lay neatly stacked to the side. It were through there they took my father.

It were far away but I could see into a dark cavern, where even then my mother lay. Dead and frozen but likely still looking herself.

While living in the miners' camp it were my job to go up above the snowline once in a while to collect the needles the men used to brew their drink. At first it were a task Little Bear and me did quick and planned liken. I weren't keen on getting hunted by those dogs again. But all the times we went back up there we never saw that gold dog or his shaggy she-dog leader again. Maybe they'd been out of their territory that day they chased us. So, after some time, we felt more at ease in the forest than anywhere else. The camp's sharp shale was grey and unappealing, but up under the forest there were a soft place to rest in the snow even if it meant enduring the gossipy whispering of the trees.

Days turned into weeks, into months and seasons. I learned my tasks better and the miners got used to me and to having camp work done for them. Little Bear grew. She reached my thigh, the height of a big dog, but much heavier. She ate a lot and the miners complained if it came from their supplies so it were another job to find her food. When I were done with the camp tidying of breakfast, some days Little Bear and I climbed down the valley where the water ran free in the river and we could catch her a fish, but only if they were running. I had to show her what to do, though I were only guessing myself. My fingers and hands were no use but I showed her the notion of how to pounce and pin a salmon to the rocky river bottom and, after some comical pantomimes I were glad there was no one to see, she got the gist of it. Her fat paws and sharp claws had much more fishing skill than my useless hands. If we brought a feed of fish back to camp, the miners looked on us favourable liken and stopped eyeing the bear suspicious and resentful.

One of the miners showed me how to set a snare for a rabbit, too. If I caught any it were first one for Little Bear and any more after that went into the miners' pot. The rabbits were running for free and it was only my labour to catch them so I thought it to be a fair deal, Little Bear being too clumsy and slow to run them down herself. Having been with me since

38

she was an infant she'd missed out on all the hunting learning she would have had from her mother. I felt bad for that and did my best to teach her what I could.

Years passed but, with the clouding over, it was always hard to tell when another season had gone by. The days got shorter until the day barely broke and then turned longer until the day lasted most of the night, and then it slowly turned again. In the old days people could note seasons by the turn of the constellations, but if the stars still hung above us we weren't to know, for they were hidden away. Little Bear went into her hibernation during the long nights, staying in our hut and not even stirring to eat. I was grateful to her for keeping my bed warm with her body heat and there weren't anything better than curling up with her when my long day of work was done.

Like up on the mountain, the cold never ceased and the sky never cleared.

As far as I could count, I saw two seasons of long nights with the miners and with regular feeding and work I, like my bear, finally grew. I made myself new clothes from the miners' cast-offs, but it were a job to mix and match the scraps to piece together something that weren't filled with holes before I started. I remembered the weaver at the chateau using a beetle found under a certain kind of rock, fried in a hot pan then crushed, to make a bright-blue dye. I used that method to give my garments a colour like pictures of the sky before the clouding over. I unravelled a woollen jumper and knitted a shawl that wrapped across my chest and tucked into my belt behind, keeping my arms free for working, and I used leather I made from rabbit skins to make that belt with a loop for my knife.

Still I kept growing. It would be a day soon when I weren't a little girl any longer.

I came to know the miners not by their names but by their habits. One was lazy and would not stir himself one bit for others. Another was a drunk who became rowdy and at times dangerous when he had a drink or ten in him. There was one who took long pulls on his pipe and seemed to live in a cloud of smoke. There was a clown, the one who told the long tales and did all the teasing and stirring, and the boss, who told them when to begin and where to dig and when to finish working for the day but did not bother himself to do much else in the way of leadership. There was one who broke up fights more than the others and another who kept himself to himself as much as possible. One was young, when put next to the rest of them, and there were three who made a group, and a sinister one at that. Those three worried me more than the rest when I felt their eyes on me as I cleared the table and filled their cups.

And it were these same three who most disliked Little Bear, even if she caught them fish, and for their own amusement they would push her into a corner and tease her until she reared on her hind legs and opened her jaws in a threat. Then they would laugh and throw things until I intervened to put a stop to such childish play. When I did they turned their attention on me with taunts about me being a feral she-bear who grew up uncivilised, my father a bear who'd lain with my mother in an unsavoury union.

I dint let their words offend me. Still, for all their callow tormenting, there was a threat underneath that I took serious liken. I were careful to lock my door from the inside when I went to bed, and keep Little Bear close. The three of them I named Leery, Surly and Sinister, and did not pass near them if I could go the long way around. These men took no satisfaction in their mining toil and grew more sour each year.

The twelfth miner was one who sometimes carried his own plate and picked up a cloth from time to time to put away dishes. His face was covered with the same bushy beard the other miners wore but he weren't as heavyset and his eyes were mild and smiled at me, though I couldn't make out his mouth to see it do the same. Sometimes after the evening meal he'd sit at the table and make drawings with a lump of cooled coal from the fire. His likenesses were good and more'n once I laughed at cruel depictions of his fellows. It seemed to me he were the odd one out of the group, having a skill such as drawing. I wondered what had brought him up here to the hard life of a miner and suspected it couldn't be anything good. Still, Little Bear let him chuck her under the chin and pat her scruff, while she stayed wary of the others. I could not have named him kind because I knew nothing of kindness at the time, but he weren't the worst and that's saying something.

The forest

It were early in the long days season when the miners loaded up the carts and took the coal crumbs down the mountain to sell. They had to pull the carts themselves, and there was always grumbling about being miners, not donkeys. But with all of them too stingy to keep a cart horse when it would be idle between trips, it were a task they set for themselves and so where was the point complaining? Still that didn't stop them.

They all went to make the sale soas to be sure of getting their fair share of the profit. And, as in other seasons, the sounds of arguing over the price and who was entitled to what share carried back up the valley long after they were out of sight.

I was not in a mood to stay in that camp while they were gone. It were bleak even without the miners and I was sick of the sight of the sink of dishes and piles of stinking washing. So in return for my work, I stole a flint and packed a sack of supplies and, with my knife tucked into my belt, Little Bear and I set off up the mountain to the forest. With my wits about me, I fixed us a cosy shelter from fallen branches and with a fire in a ring of stones we had a contented camp in the shush of the forest.

I'd scraped and stretched the she-bear fur, setting it to cure proper, so now it were warm and light about my head and shoulders. I wore it like a hood, a hole for my face underneath the she-bear's muzzle. Her furry ears sat atop my own skull and I knew there were no senses left in them, but somehow I imagined the noises of the forest sharpened having them there.

Now it seemed that a rustle of chatter went through the treetops when Little Bear and I arrived in the forest, and instead of tittle-tattling, the trees seemed pleased to see us. It might have been my fancy but the branches appeared to close in over our heads and protect us from heavier falls of snow. And did they whisper their pride when I snared a rabbit and set it roasting? I settled on it not being of significance whether it were true or my own imagination, because the idea was enough to please me.

While Little Bear slept in our shelter and I sat quiet in the snow, all manner of bird life stepped out to inspect our camp. There were bold green parrots that climbed on my shelter, picking at loose parts with their long curved beaks, as if inspecting its structure and finding it wanting. And there were fantails and tomtits, too, in the understorey. They called to one another as they worked, sharing their business in a companionable way that set my heart feeling lonely for family. Some of them as small as insects they were, some larger. The ones with black helmets and round yellow bellies tilted their tiny heads to the side to look at me, pitiful like, for being all on my own. Where were my fellows? they seemed to wonder.

One day I wandered near a rocky outcrop, attracted by cheeping, and found a nest of young falcons in a simple scrape on the ground. I did not touch them, but for my trouble was dived upon savagely by the mother returning from her hunt. Away a safe distance I admired her elegant wingspan and the markings that gave her an everlasting fierce glare. Using a cool coal from my fire I marked my own brow the same way.

We walked up the mountain until we came upon the upper run of the river that passed by the miners' camp and followed it a ways, just from curiosity. Little Bear and I stuck to the higher banks, walking among tussocks of grass patched with snow. It felt fine to stretch my legs. My breath came out in white puffs and the cloud cover hung so low it were almost like I could reach up and brush it with my fingertips. The higher we went, the slower the flow, and soon we reached the glacier that fed the river. It were a sight to see. Giant ice boulders, some tinged a bright aqua blue, some an icy white, still flowing like water but in their own slow time. I dint dare walk among them for fear I'd be standing beneath when one crashed down the frozen flow.

Upriver something caught my eye. Climbing up to inspect closer, I found what looked to be the mouth of an old mine, its entrance partly fallen in. The mountains were full of such holes, dark and damp inside with the air holding onto the disappointment of men who'd hoped to strike it rich. And not only their disappointment remained but often their bones as well for it were dangerous and unstable work. It weren't uncommon for quakes to come up through the earth, shaking the mountain as if it were trying to rid itself of the tunnelling creatures, burying men where they dug.

Sitting to the side of the entrance were iron drums, the paint that once coated them in bright warning colours now faded. Little Bear sat on her haunches and put her nose in the air, sniffing, and then backed away. I couldn't smell whatever it was that offended her but I could see one drum had been punctured low down, the ground now damp with whatever had leaked out. Carefully avoiding stepping in the muck, I went close to the edge and could see below that the tumble of glacier ice were stained with the viscous liquid.

Just then an icy gust of air blew out through the mine tunnel, catching me between my shoulder blades, like a door swinging shut.

The entrance to the mine remained a black hole. 'Likely the gates of hell closing down in there somewhere,' I murmured to Little Bear, sinking my hand into her scruff for comfort. 'Let's get out of here.'

It were the trees that told me of the miners' return. They saw the men from on high, trundling the empty carts up the valley, and passed along the message to me that it were time to go back to my duties in camp. How I received this message, I don't fully know. I just know I heard a whisper. And sure enough, when Little Bear and I emerged at the treeline and looked down the valley, we could see smoke rising and movement back in the camp. We hurried down the mountain then for I did not want to attract attention to my wandering. So we cut around the back and over the ridge and came into camp that way.

I could sense something amiss as soon as I stepped foot among the huts. The miners, instead of paying me no mind at all, seemed to fall quiet and look at me sidelong. I put it down to the coal on my brow that I had forgotten to rinse off in the river, but even after I'd cleaned my face, there was an unnatural hush over the table as I set out food and filled their cups that evening. It made my cheeks flush as I felt eyes on me when my back were turned. I worried that my theft of the flint had been discovered and felt a swelling of anger in my chest. If I weren't entitled to a small payment for my years of service, then there weren't a bunch of meaner-spirited men in all the land than these. I swung around to confess my crime and claim the flint as rightfully mine, but before I opened my mouth, Surly rocked back on his chair, picking his teeth.

'Girl, my hairy smackmouth mate here spoke to a man who spoke to a man who says you're a runaway. And there's a reward for your whereabouts being made known.' He gave a sly glance at his fellows around the long table. 'The woman who calls herself Rain up on the mountain where you says you come from wants you back. Says you belong with her.'

I'd seen for myself that, while taciturn when sober, the miners could talk up a mountain of rubbish when they were full of alcohol. One of them, full of drink in the city, must have boasted they took in a girl to work for them for none but room and board. I dint want to imagine what else would have been said about my person, but it seemed it were enough to pique some curiosity. I saw now my whole stay in the miners' camp had been a loan of time I now owed interest on. Even with their infrequent trips to the city and me being of no particular interest except as unpaid labour until now, it had been only but a matter of time til word got to my stepmother that I were still alive.

The hunter may have fooled her with the she-bear's heart, but not forever. Had he confessed to letting me live? I wondered what had been his fate. Nothing good, I imagined. Perhaps I'd already been released from my foolish betrothal.

Surly rocked forward and set his elbows back to the table with a bump. I backed away and held onto the bench behind me with fingertips.

'It's a tidy sum of cash she's offeren. Me and the others here discussed all the way back up the accursed valley whetheren to return you back where you came from.'

My eyes skittered around the seated miners. Some wouldn't meet my gaze, keeping their glances to the hands in their laps or making a show of being preoccupied with brushing coal dust from the sleeves of their coats. Some looked back at me but I could tell they were undecided on the matter of turning me in. They paid me none for my labour and were already remembering the fights over whose turn it was to wash the dishes. The tidy sum that Surly was referring to would have to be shared, and it's a large amount that stands splitten twelve ways and still comes out sounding tempting.

Little Bear was looking to me for reassurance, sensing with her animal mind the tension in the room. She started ambling over from her nook in the corner to stand by my side but I waved her back by flicken my fingers. She knew enough to stay put then. I didn't want to aggravate the situation by bringing a grown bear to my side of the conversation. Surly and Sinister were twitchy enough as it were. And still I hadn't said anything to my defence. What's the point? I thought. I could see that all the looking aside and fidgeting meant that the decision had already been made coming up the mountain. There was nothing I could say to change it now.

Bushy Beard stood and placed his large working hands flat on the table.

'We agreed that she's worth more to us here for the long days, and the reward int going nowhere. It'll still be there at the end of the season when we next go down the mountain. We'll take her with us then and seeabouts how much that reward has increased by in the meantime. Int none of us turning round to be making that blasting trip again right now, am I right?'

It were a long trip down to the city. It took them a week there and back. A week of sleeping outdoors on cold hard ground and in between taking their turn easing heavy carts downhill, which int easy, then hauling them filled with supplies back up, which is exhausting. They always came in with sore heads from all the drinking they got to in town, and I could see the leftover quease Surly and Sinister were feeling from the stinking strong town booze by the leavings on their plates. Still sick to their stomachs they were and cranky with it. It also left them weak of resolve.

'I say she keeps on at her work, and we let that reward mature into something worth the dividing,' Bushy Beard said.

And so he had the last word that day and it held for a few weeks more. There was coal to be dug out of the dark damp tunnels and the miners returned to their toil. Most days they were too tired and it were too cold for them to wash the black dust from their faces before dinner so they sat at table like demons dug from the firey guts of the earth. Just the whites of their eyes and the yellow of their teeth showed in the dim lamp light. My face must have looked the same for the air were filled with the same sooty dust and it rose from the washing tubs on laundry day. It collected in the grain of my skin giving me the look of black blood running in my veins. And worse, it caught in my lungs, giving me the same dry cough the men had at the end of a long day.

Filling the water barrels from the river and dragging them up the valley were heavy work, too heavy for me, so it were shared between the men. One day I paused in my work for it were Smoky hauling the cart and while I watched he coughed and spluttered his way through camp, hawking and spitting what he brought up. It weren't pretty to watch and so I went about my business, coming out after cleaning the next hut to see the miner parking the cart of water barrels and then bending over, like he had a cramp in his belly. I paid him no mind, having plenty to do and no time to waste on sympathy. After a time anyway, he straightened up, lit his pipe and passed across the way.

That evening the camp had run out of the pine needle beer the miners usually drank. It was a sour-smelling liquid, dark and sticky with a bitterness that turned my mouth inside-out when I were unwise enough to give it a taste. The miner who made it I named Brewer and he was being upbraided for the next batch not being ready yet.

'Where's our beer, you lazy blaster?'

'Shut yer ugly gob. It int ready on account of the unseasonal ficking cold,' replied Brewer.

'It's always cold on this arse-around island, that's no excuse. You're sod-lazy, is the sum total of it.'

'Shut your blasting mouth, you pile of shet! You should be getting down on your knees and thanking me for the steady supply of ale instead a piling abuse on me for the temporary lack of it. The beer won't blasting brew if it int warm enough!'

This exchange would have come to blows ifen the boss hadn't slammed his open palm on the table and brought the argument to a close. After some further grumbling the miners settled for plain water with their meal. I noticed Smoky weren't at table and overheard one of the men saying he had a bellyache and were sleeping it off in his cabin.

But by the end of the meal Smoky weren't the only one with a bellyache. One by one the miners pushed their plates away and sat back, turning white and some of them green. Brewer began coughing and a rag held to his mouth came away stained with blood.

Seeing this, Sinister shouted at me, 'You poisoned us, you witch!'

I were confused. It's a fact I weren't a master cook but over the years I had muddled my way into serving up food that didn't attract more than the usual amount of whining. This night were no different. I hadn't used any new ingredients and none of it had been rank or rotten going in.

'It weren't my cooking,' I said in my defence.

The boss, picking up his water and sniffing it, took out a match and held it under his cup. Soon the unmistakable odour of rotten eggs rose from the contents. 'It's the water,' he said. 'It be tainted.'

Sinister lurched from his seat, hand clutched to the pain in his side there. 'We shoulda thrown the cursed girl out when we first laid eyes on her. She done nothen but cause discontent in this camp since she arrived. And now she's blasting poisoned our water to kill us.' Staggering, because of the twisting in his guts, he backed me into a corner of the mess. Little Bear, at my side, stood on her hind legs and opened her jaws in a threat. I pulled on her scruff to set her down, thinking desperately.

What had caused the river to be poisoned? It looked to flow clean and clear and strong as it always had. Then I remembered the old drum at the mine, punctured and leaking its contents onto the head of the glacier. Were it possible the offer of a reward were just my stepmother's way of flushing out information about where I were hiding? If so, it had worked. Rain must be losing what were left of her senses to poison a whole river just for the chance of killen me. If it were as I suspected, though, that is exactly what she'd done. But if I were to tell the miners my suspicions, I'd also be tellen them of my wandering far and high in their absence.

Sinister were still sneering and Little Bear, showing her teeth too, was eager to sink them into whatever sour-tasting part of him she could get to. The nuggety miner, backing off a little, swiped a knife from the table. It were only good for spreading butter, but by now the other miners were on their feet and gathering around to see. I had no choice.

'Wait, wait!' I said. 'I saw an old drum leaking into the glaciers, way up. Above the snowline,' I added reluctantly. 'It looked to have been drilled into recent liken. I dint think anything of it at the time but Little Bear weren't keen on the smell. It must've been my stepmother's work. She's heard I'm here. She's tryen to kill me and cheat you of the reward,' I finished, hoping that mentioning the money they were banking on might remind them I was worth not killen right then and there.

'How dare she give us the bellyache?' Leery said. 'Who does that crazy woman think she is, giving us rotten guts? Our work is back-breaking enough without suffering the agony of a wire-brush going through our innards.'

'Killen a whole river, it int right,' the boss said, bent over his guts and wheezing.

'Makes me of an opinion we should keep the girl awhile longer out of the stuck-up blasting woman's sight and increase the price of that reward,' another said.

'Fact she wants the girl dead don't inspire confidence she's going to be handing out rewards for her safe return, you gorm- less deadheads,' the boss said through gritted teeth.

'Could be we send her a message, sayen we got the girl and stop killen us?' the youngest miner, Junior, suggested.

'And who'll carry this message?' asked Bushy Beard, who weren't suffering the cramps in his belly as much as the others. 'You got a bird trained to carry messages in the old way hidden somewhere?' He addressed the miners in general. 'Not been any satphones hereabouts recently that I've seen. Lessen you have one stashed under your hairy arse?'

Junior, offended, glared at Bushy Beard but did not reply.

'Then maybe kill her ourselfs and deliver her head up yon mountain,' grunted Rowdy, the drunk, bent over double from the pain.

'And arrive begging for a reward like a stinking rat-dog? Job's done for her then, pig-breath. All she does is thank us through her locked gates and send us away. Besides, I'm not one for wading up mountains through waist-deep blasting snow,' Leery said.

There the discussion paused while men clutched their guts and writhed in agony. I stayed quiet, even while they proposed detaching my head from my shoulders.

The room fell silent, except for the ones with gold in their eyes, Leery and Sinister in the main, who weren't easily willing to give up the hopes of being rich, even if it were only briefly. Bushy Beard joined their whispering and I worried their decision on me and my future was not going to be to my liking.

Surly rose to his feet then and, swallowing queasily, stated the terms. 'No more wanderen up in the forest, girl,' he said, pointing his thick crooked first finger at me. 'Next chance we get we're taking you to the city to sell to the highest bidder. And the blasting bear stays chained,' he added final.

And because he feared her, he pulled a thick leather collar from a sack he had about him and made me fix it round Little Bear's neck. It connected to a long chain that he took one end of and pulled my bear behind him out the door.

I followed along, using all the curse words I'd learned from the miners' filthy mouths over the seasons, directing all of them at Surly and Sinister, who helped with dragging Little Bear, while she sat on her haunches and roared in protest. The two of them hammered a stout stake into the open ground in camp and locked the chain around it, while poor Little Bear looked to me in confusion, walking til her chain pulled tight and yanked her back. Her mouth opened and she cried out.

I had to cease my cursing then because my throat closed over and tears poured down my cheeks and, to my shame, I started begging the miners to let her off.

'She's not going to hurt any one of you,' I said. 'I'll make sure of it. Just please set her free. She don't know what it means to be chained. It'll break her spirit and turn her mean.'

'She's already mean,' Sinister said, 'to most but you. She's a blasting wild animal. Int no place in a human camp for a wild animal. Besides,' he added with a sneer, 'she stays chained, you're as good as chained too. We know you int going nowhere without your precious bear.'

And he were right. All thoughts of getting my furs and running for the forest at the first possible chance that came along flew from my head. I fell to my knees on the sharp scree.

The miners had followed us out of the mess to watch the spectacle and now they turned from me. There were some who I'd believed weren't bad all the way through and I called to them, trying to remember what they called each other, to make my appeals. But one by one they shook their heads. Some I could tell weren't in full agreement with the means but still they had to stand together to make the ends.

Bushy Beard was the last to leave. 'I did all I could,' he said to me through his thick whiskers. 'They wanted to do worse and I talked em down from that. So think on it. And speaken of worse, I'll have your knife, if you please.'

It weren't a request.

I pulled it from my belt and hurled it past his head so it stuck in the cabin wall, twenty paces away. I'd been practising this skill up in the forest and it gave me considerable satisfaction watching a look of surprise pass over Bushy Beard's face. But seeing as he'd gotten his way, and I'd not only lost my knife but also given away a secret, I was kicking myself when it were said and done.

He pulled my knife from the wood and closed the door behind him. The miners one by one staggered off into the darkness to their cabins to groan the night through.

I stayed with Little Bear, my arms wrapped around her neck, through the cold evening and into the night until I were chilled to my bones, even with her warmth beside me. There was no way I could survive even the short night out in the open yard like that, so before long I had to leave my bear and go to my hut. I held her snout in my hands and looked in her eyes and did my best to explain.

'I gotta go inside, Little Bear,' I told her through my chattering teeth. 'I don't want to leave you but if I don't I'm going to freeze and be no use to you dead.'

There's no understanding using words between people and animals but they get the idea well enough using other means. She saw and smelled I were sorry and cold but she couldn't make sense of why she were chained. So when I started to walk away toward my hut she followed until her bonds brought her up short. And when I kept on, she cried at me to take her with me and it were all I could do not to go back to her and let death creep up while I slept. But that would leave Little Bear chained up for good, and I couldn't do that to her. For now, this was the best I could do and I forced my feet into a walk to bed.

I thanked the hidden stars I had not taken any of the water from the afternoon's fetching. Nor had I given any to Little Bear. So we were spared the agonies of the night. However I were forced to bear witness to them by hearing all the groaning and retching and worse going on through the camp. Still, my sympathies were not stirred. At one point during the night I heard my door being locked from the outside, and that made me even madder. It seemed to me that the miners were getting some of the justice that had been a long time coming to them. Locking me up, chaining my bear and forcing me to work against my will. No, whatever bellyaches they were suffering were due to them and more.

It were the coldest and loneliest night of my cold and lonely life so far. Little Bear and me could do nothing together but both cry ourselves to sleep.

Even when I were shut in my tower room by myself all those years, wasting away slowly, I never felt sad or wretched. The injustice of my imprisonment burned like a fire in my belly so I never fell over into misery. I were also young, just a child mostly, who didn't hardly know any better. I woke and ate and slept and in between let my mind wander to stories I'd been told, followed the light as it crossed the floor, or conversed with passing mice. My body were locked up but my mind was free to roam as it liked.

Now it were different. Now I felt my mind become a slow gluey mess.

I were despairing.

It took a few days, but the miners one by one recovered and went back to work, looking peaky and stepping gingerly down the valley back to the mine. The poisoning would've been enough to finish me I dint doubt, but the miners were made of tough gristle all the way through and it would take more'n that to murder them.

It were now my task to collect snow and boil it for water which was more work added to the pile I already had. I had to rise even earlier and had less time to sit with my bear giving her company, the only thing that lifted her head. But if there was a good side to the miners being poisoned it were that they now felt bitter toward my stepmother, instead of me.

They unlocked my door when they left for the day and I was expected to do my work without leaving the camp boundaries.

Those that used to lift a finger for themselves made no effort anymore so every task was left to me. Each hut had to be tidied and straightened, beds made, floors swept, washing collected. When that were done there was the evening meal and the next day's breakfast to be prepared, too.

And I had to go about my work being tormented by the sight of my bear on a chain.

At first, Little Bear tried to follow me as I passed, always being reminded of her confinement with a jolt. It broke my heart every time. But it hurt even more when she stopped. Instead of coming to me for a greeting, she turned away, lying on the ground and not showing any interest in the food I brought her. She lost weight. It were the long days season so she had come out of her hibernating and she should have been feeding up, putting on muscle and fat, but I couldn't go hunting or fishing for her anymore, forbidden as I was from leaving camp. And besides, I were without my knife, and there were nothing coming into camp volunteering to be Little Bear's dinner.

I tried all I could to free her but the miners knew their metal fixings. The stake were hammered in deep and the chain was tight at both ends, with a padlock on the thick collar Little Bear wore. I eyed the key hanging at Surly's side a hundred times a night as I served the miners at their table, wishing it would jump into my hand. Meanwhile, I weren't sure what Bushy Beard had done with my knife. I'd searched his cabin and not found it, and if he carried it on his person, it were hid well away.

Sinister and Leery had started to not just harass me with their looks but with their filthy hands as well. Leery would grab me by my hips and lean in whispering with his stinken breath until I wrenched myself away, only to get my wrist caught by Sinister, who would pull me in close and run his other hand over my backside. There were nothing I could do to get away with my wrist caught in his miner's grasp. It were the grip he used all the long day on pick and shovel digging under a mountain. I had no hope of getting away. So I used my eyes and fixed them on the boss, pleaden like. Eventually he would slam his fist onto the table, making all the dishes jump, and snarl for Sinister to release me soas I could fill his glass.

One night when I were finally done with the stack of greasy washing from the evening meal, I walked slowly through the thick black of the night to my hut. Feeling the way with my senses for want of a lamp, which weren't to be wasted on me, I was set upon suddenly from behind by two miners. They must have been waiting for me in the dark.

They pushed me against my hut, pressing my face hard into the boards. It were too dark to discover which they were by looking at their faces and they all smelled as bad as each other so the stench filling my nostrils was no help either. There were rough hands all over me. My hips were grabbed and my feet kicked apart. My heart raced and I whimpered, ashamed to call out. Anyway, what help was there to come?

There was a part of me, even while I struggled in the miners' iron grip, that were amazed it hadn't happened til now. But I told that part of my mind, firm and sharp, to shut the hell up. I had to do something to make it harder for them to get their way.

So I fought.

I squirmed and kicked and bit anything I could get my teeth

to. I brought my knees up to my chest and rolled to one side then the other. I crawled away when I got the chance, only to be gripped by the ankle and pulled back once again. But I kept fighting. The life of a camp slave weren't for no gain and now I really were strong for my small size. Still, fighting was tiring. Slowly I was pinned down, like a butterfly on a board. I could feel one of them, getting a hold on my wrist and pressing it to my chest, grunting under his breath with the effort, his stinking groins pressed against mine.

I turned my face away in disgust and gazed blindly into the dark of the cloud-covered night, thinking to take my mind somewhere out of my body. Then I caught the gleam of a pair of eyes glowing red in the dark. There came a growling, low and fearsome, but audible even over the miners' wheezing and grunting. My assailants froze, looking around, their animal instincts coming alert too. Now in my side vision I could see three dogs, maybe more, advancing slowly between the huts, one step at a time, heads held low in menacing stalking stance, lips pulled back in snarls.

The miners left off their hold on me and, swearing softly, fumbled under their clothes for weapons. Finding none, being set upon the assault of a girl, not fighting wild dogs, when leaving for their night's activities, now their only option was retreat. They backed away slowly, turning to run like the craven sooks they were when they were far enough away from the dogs' red eyes.

I stayed where I were.

The lead dog came up level with me and I kept my eyes cast down, soas not to challenge him. There were not much I could do if he meant to make me his dinner, with my legs folded under me and my heart racing from not one bad fright but two. Peeking from the corners of my eyes, though, I made out a golden coat.

It were hard to know, but that dog might have been the young one we were running from that day when Little Bear and I arrived in the camp. If it were he'd grown and filled out. His coat were shaggy, especially in a ruff around his neck, and his paws were almost as large as Little Bear's. His ears stood up, set on a large round skull, and he'd lost the innocence he'd had that day when I'd charged him wearing the she-bear fur. It dint seem like now there'd be anything much that would take him by surprise. Not even a girl dressed as a bear.

He looked me over with his superior senses in the dark and I held out my hand, thinking to thank him. But being a wild dog, he weren't interested in pats, and passed off mine like it meant nothing to him. Then he backed away and he and his pack mates were gone.

I raised myself up and hobbled to my cabin, setting my pawed-over clothes back to straight. It were a lucky escape. I spent the rest of the night trembling and wiping away tears of fright.

After that I looked forward to hearing the lock of my door turn from the outside, because at times there were others who came and tried the catch in the dark of night, rattling my door and, finding it fast, cursing quiet and creeping away. It were then I realised that Bushy Beard were still doing me favours, though it didn't feel much like one, being made a prisoner again.

The ice-storm

>>———>

Soon after being attacked I paused in my work one day and looked up. The sky was closed over by thick white cover as it always were but to the south the grey was darker, with clouds piling up on one another. The breeze chilled and stiffened as I went about the camp. A storm coming in. Squalls from the south were bitter cold and brought a freeze. By morning the camp would be covered with thick ice on every surface it found. There would likely be wind too, howling round the cabins and sweeping loose items away. It weren't my job to tidy away tools or any of the building materials kept around camp so, even though I saw things likely to come loose, I did nothing to move them or tie them down.

Little Bear were a wee bit brighter that day than I usually found her. She raised her head and let me chuck under her chin and stroke her ears. I stayed well clear of her scruff as the tight leather collar chafed and she weren't above snapping at me if I passed my hand too close to her sore parts. All I could do was squeeze salted water on the rawness to keep it clean, though she didn't thank me for the sting it caused her. I sighed and checked to see if any of the fastenings had come loose since I last looked. Finding it all as tight and hopeless as always, I left her to do my work.

All the long afternoon the wind picked up and the temperature dropped. I kept the fire stoked in the mess and prepared the evening meal. The miners came in chilled and more worn out than usual, having to lean into the wind coming back up the valley and burning through energy keeping warm. They kept their eyes on their plates and finished without delay, retiring to their beds as soon as they were done. Through fatigue and carelessness it were this night that Bushy Beard left his coat in the mess after he went to his bed. I were busy clearing the table and setting the room back to rights so I didn't notice it straight away but when my eye fell upon it I couldn't cross the room fast enough to rifle through the pockets, looking for my knife.

And there it were, in an inner pocket. Once it were back in my hand again, the bone handle with its strange markings sitting heavy in my palm, my mind fired up from the gluey mess it had been since Little Bear were chained up. Thoughts and ideas piled up on top of one another, like I couldn't get thinking fast enough. It were only a few seconds before I knew what was to be done.

First I tucked my knife into my belt, then I took a sack and filled it with food, as much as I could fit without being too bulky to travel fast. I felt pressed for time for Bushy Beard could notice his oversight at any moment and make his way back for his coat. He knew for sure I wouldn't miss a chance to get my knife. And he also knew I were desperate to get my bear out of chains.

With the wind howling around the camp even stronger now,

it were a battle to get the door of the mess closed behind me, and then it took all my strength to cross the open ground to Little Bear. She were curled in a ball to keep warm but I started whispering my plan and fancied I saw her ear flick toward me. Ifen she didn't understand my words, she had her other animal senses to help her figure out we were leaving. I took my knife and, under the cover of the blowing wind and sleet that were slicing through camp, started hacking through Little Bear's collar. It were a job to saw through that thick leather, even though Bushy Beard had kept my blade sharp, and it were hurting Little Bear's raw scruff to do it but I kept up whispering we were leaven and she stayed still and let me work at it.

I had a couple of inches left when a gust of wind sent some loose timbers flying across the way, slamming into the cabins. A weak spirit light came up and I had to crouch down behind Little Bear in case I were seen. Lucky for us another few almighty gusts of gale followed the first and ifen the miner thought he were coming out to fix anything down, he changed his mind.

And then what I'd been afraid of happened. A light appeared in Bushy Beard's cabin, the last one on the edge of camp, and I saw his door come open and he bent into the wind to make his way to the mess. He'd remembered his coat and were heading to retrieve it. My hut was up the other way, at the end of camp nearest the forest.

'Little Bear, you stay right here. I'm comen back for you,' I told her and, stayen low, I pelted to my cabin and grabbed my meagre possessions. It was mainly my she-bear fur I couldn't do without, but gloves and my woollen shawl would give me the best chance of seeing out an ice-storm in the open. I were in and out of my cabin as quick as I could, but it weren't quick enough, because I saw Bushy Beard spot me, even through the swirling wind and snow.

'Girl, you halt there ifen you know what's good for you,' he said, and then he bellowed, 'Miners! The girl's escapen!'

But his words were snatched away as they left his mouth by the howling wind. Again he called for help, deeper this time so it carried better, and he caught a lull in the gale. This time his words reached the ears he'd intended. Doors began to open.

Bushy Beard approached me slowly, like I were the cornered bear, and I pulled out my knife, feeling its handle familiar in my palm. It were sharp, I knew that, even after sawing through my bear's collar, but I was out of practice with my throwing. Even so, this was my chance to leave, and I weren't letting it go easy. I was on the edge of camp, the valley rising behind me, up through tussock country to the snowline where I knew I'd find shelter under the forest. But Little Bear were still fastened, and now the miners were gathering behind Bushy Beard, standing between me and my bear, two inches of leather still holding her to the stake.

'Easy there,' Bushy Beard said, slowly coming toward me.

I raised my knife. 'Stay back or I'll stick this in your ribs,' I called, loud as I could. 'You know I can.'

'Girl, you're not going to live through the night, let alone the rest of your life, in the forest,' Bushy Beard said. 'You can stay here. We'll let your bear off her chain ifen it's what you want.'

'You're lying.'

'We can't do without you around here. We know that.'

I scoffed. It weren't going to get him anywhere tellen me what I already knew.

'Curse you all, you ungrateful pigs,' I yelled. 'I worked for years for you and all for none but abuse and chainen my bear.'

'Girl, if it weren't for our shelter you'd be dead and you know it,' said Sinister, creeping up beside Bushy Beard.

Fury burned in my belly. I owed them nothing for the shelter because I'd paid for it a hundred times over with my work.

'My name isn't *girl*. I'm Snow. And I swear, afore your life is done, you'll have cause to finally remember it,' I shouted over the howl of the wind.

Even as I let loose my curse, I knew I was wasting time by stopping to argue. The other miners had gathered at Bushy Beard's back, the whole motley crew of them, standing between me and my bear and now slowly moving toward me. I couldn't kill them all with my knife throwing, so my only option was to turn and run. My heart broke clean in two at having to make the choice but with the wind throwing hail like sharp pellets in my face it was all I could do to keep my head down and put one foot in front of the other to make headway.

As I ran a big gust came up and I heard the sound of tearing metal in the camp, the miners all yelling at each other behind me. And then I heard a sound that chilled me and fired hope in my heart at the same time: Little Bear roaring at full volume. I turned, and through the flying sleet I could see my bear on her hind legs, now taller than all of the short-statured miners who had broken their cover to gather around her, holding picks and shovels aimed her way. She bounced down on her front legs and reared again, bringing the full force of her weight to the collar at her neck and the chain at the stake.

And she were free. Just like that. She broke through the last two inches of leather holding her with pure strength. She could hardly believe it herself, I could tell, but she didn't stop and instead scattered the miners in her path with a snap of her huge teeth and ran toward me through the ice-storm.

When she reached me she kept on past.

She were done with me and my traitorous ways. She was flying back to the forest to find some of her own kind, finished with faithless girls.

What were I thinking, even considering leaving her? I thought. My only friend in the world.

But when she was a ways in front my bear turned and I saw that she held no grudge after all and were breaking trail for me through the snow which was falling fast and already knee deep.

What are you waiting for? she seemed to say.

We ran. Slogging through the storm to get as far away from the stench of the miners' camp as we could. My breath burned in my throat and my legs ached with the effort. But my exertion kept me warm and it was so cold that standing still I would have frozen to death in minutes. After we cleared the furthest reaches of the camp, we kept going. As long as one foot fell in front of the other, I knew we'd get to the forest eventually. And even though I were chilled on the outside and soon worn through with fatigue, joy burned inside me that my bear and I were free again.

Me and Little Bear pushed into the gale the whole night long. She broke a trail and I followed as best I could, frozen though my feet and hands soon were. Around dawn we passed over tussock country and back under the shelter of the forest where the wind weren't so fierce. Still, the falling snow was deep enough and soft enough to just about swallow us up. The ice-storm was helpful for covering our tracks soon after we left them but it were no secret we'd head for the forest and I didn't want to lay down only to be easily picked up again by the miners at first light. So we kept on until we reached the very tallest trees where the canopy overhead almost closed the sky out above and none but the lightest of snowfall filtered all the way to the ground. There I judged it safe enough to rest awhile, and with branches above to obscure the smoke, I made a fire with my flint and pine needles and Little Bear and I lay down exhausted.

I couldn't rest until I had slipped out of wet boots and gloves and held my hands to thaw at the fire. When feeling returned I considered it safe enough to sleep without risk of waken up with frostbitten fingers and toes. It was a deep sleep I fell into, filled with dreams of being chased, with my legs frozen into useless blocks that refused to move. I reached out to Little Bear and remembered that I was outside and the only real sounds were the creaking and whispering of the forest. Then I slept again until the same dreams chased me awake.

The rising light of day quietened the ice-storm and when I opened my eyes it was calm in the treetops. The deepest hush settled onto the forest floor, so that even the crackle of my fire seemed loud enough to lead the miners to our camp. I built up my flames using pinecones and broken branches until I could melt some snow and drink a cup of hot water.

'That were a lucky escape,' I told my bear. 'I'm never going to get stuck in that kind of confinement again, you hear me? Better to stay away from people and live our lives under the sky.'

My bear rested her head on her paws in agreement. I ran

my hand through her thick brown scruff. I were determined to keep my bear free and felt nothing but happy to be on our own once again. But a thought nagged at me. How long could a girl live alone in a forest?

In the days and weeks following our escape we lived quiet, hunting rabbits and fishing in a river that weren't the one poisoned by my stepmother, and camping wherever we chose. Little Bear recovered her good spirits and showed me she were glad we were free and held no resentment toward me. Animals for certain have a memory but unlike people they are more concerned with the present and tend to live there rather than the past. What was done was gone and Little Bear bore me no ill will.

It took me longer to shed my resentment. We'd been abused by the miners and for no wrongdoing on our part. But being bitter gives you wrinkles, Cook told me, so I tried to think of what I'd gained. I'd taught myself how to hunt and fish and throw a knife. Also how to cook and clean for twelve men. Although I didn't plan on doing that again while warm blood flowed through my veins.

Little Bear and I roamed, walking up the craggy mountainsides to look out from the tops and get our bearings. We crossed all manner of landscapes: the slippery shale cliffs, which we tried to stay away from because of the lack of cover, through soft yellow and purple tussock fields, down into green valleys through wisps of low cloud. But always we returned back above the snowline and under cover of the forest. To the north was the coast and the city where the miners went to sell their coal. To the west their camp. To the south my stepmother's chateau. I kept east soas to be out of reach but this kept me well into high country, with alpine heights at my back where even in the long days it were too cold to go. Even so there was a wide range of country Little Bear and I could call our own if we felt of a mind to.

There used to be trails in those parts, with huts, and we came upon these now and again. Most were old and fallen down with only animals making use of the shelter. Some were in better repair and it were tempting to set myself down in one. I thought of patching the roof and sweeping out the dust of years. Little Bear and and I could last out the long nights in that kind of shelter. But being placed on trails it weren't only me who'd happened on these huts over the years. I could always tell from fresh ashes in the stoves, or footprints on the dusty floors. Some left a mess, others tidied up and even left a gift. I'd have not minded my path crossing with the ones that left pinecones for setting the next fire; it were the ones that broke the windows for nothing and left their leavings in a mess I dint want to meet.

In other parts of the high country old boardwalks crossed over wetlands and bridges ran high over streams. Most of these were broken down and too much of a hazard to use. Sometimes I'd walk out on a swing bridge, seeing about testing it for walking over to save myself a longabouts way round, but even if I'd been willing to chance it, Little Bear would have none of rope crossings, sitting on her haunches, turning back her ears and giving me a look like I'd lost my mind. So we'd go the longaways down into the gully, get wet feet crossing the river, and then make the hard slog back uphill.

I had Little Bear to talk to but she weren't in the habit of saying much back. She had her way of letting me know when I was going off on a rave, turning her ears away from my voice and shaking her head like a fly had crawled into her ear. Embarrassed, I'd shut my mouth for a while. She had a lot to teach me about thinking and not thinking, my bear. To me it seemed like she spent her days with a glorious clear head, her thoughts only starting up when she was hungry or tired. Then she'd have some ideas about how to attend to those needs and once that were done, she'd go quiet again. I think my talk disturbed her placid pool of thoughts and that were when she'd turn to me with a look that seemed to say, Snow, that's enough now. And I'd do my best to breathe slow and easy and put my thoughts into one foot in front of the other for a time. Little Bear were pleased with me when I could keep this up. Slowly I learned to do it for longer and longer. But that dint mean there weren't times when I had to clear my mind by speaking my thoughts aloud. And most of these times Little Bear seemed to listen politely. Like a good friend who'd heard it all before but were kind enough to hear it again ifen it made me feel better.

Mainly what was on my mind was how to find a life to live. It was Little Bear's opinion that this was living; walking around the forest, finding food, sleeping. And I were happy too for a time. I was free, with none telling me what to do or how to do it and when. But being free left room for other thoughts to crowd in. Like how were it fair that I live my life hidden away in the high country soas I didn't get kild by my nasty stepmother? And there was unfinished business in the miners' camp, too. It weren't necessary to chain my bear and threaten to turn me in for a reward. I weren't something that

70

could be bought and sold for another's profit. The price on my head came to bother me. I couldn't go east or west or north or south, so how was I really free? And for all the good of Little Bear's peaceful company, I had the feeling that there must be others walking on two legs who were worth knowing.

If I thought about it carefully and laid out twigs in the snow to keep count, I reckoned this to be the fifteenth long days season of my life. At sixteen I would come of age, and then I'd be able to claim my father's property as he'd told me. This is what my stepmother feared all along. I could hide up in the forest for the rest of my life, or I could make a plan to take back what was mine.

I hadn't forgotten either about my betrothal to the hunter. Though I were a child at the time I made the promise, it dint feel right to be hiding away from it. It needed clearing away.

The trader

There were two trails Little Bear and I steered our way around careful liken because there were sometimes people to be seen travelling them. Mostly they were traders, loaded up with goods, sometimes leading a small horse carrying more packs than was kind. As we went on our rounds, checking our rabbit traps, we passed a point where we looked down on one of the byways, and I always looked for travellers, stopping awhile to watch. The novelty of another human, even if it were a wiley old trader four and more times my age, was enough to catch my interest. Sometimes they let scraps of bright fabrics trail from their packs, or tied bells to a pony's bridle, soas to signal their coming to potential buyers. It made me sorely tempted to run down the pass to meet them and run those pretty silks through my fingers, but I had no money, only rabbit furs to trade.

One day I couldn't resist. From high up, the trader looked to me like the oldest of men, bent over from the weight of his pack, and picking his way over the trail at the slowest pace

I'd seen yet. He pulled a donkey behind who looked almost as ancient, and who had to pause between steps soas to keep pace with his tortoise master.

'Stay here,' I told my bear and, leaving my she-bear fur, began slipping down the shale slope to meet the trader before he left the valley floor. As it was, my eagerness meant I landed on the flat well ahead of him. The trader was bent over from the weight of his pack and the bells of his donkey disguised my steps, so when I called out a hail I startled him almost to death.

'Good almighty, girl, where'd you spring from?' he said, turning as best he could under the hump of his pack to scan the brown-grey rocks on the slopes above us. I didn't worry he would see Little Bear for she were likely asleep and looking like a boulder by now.

He looked at me with keen sharp eyes, head tipped like a bird. 'You look to be from the islands. Are you a Voyager? Where're your people?'

I dint answer whereabouts I'd come from, instead saying, 'May I look at your wares, trader?'

The old man looked uncertain. 'I don't fancy stoppen right here,' he said. 'I've a ways to go afore I set down my pack today. And besides,' he said, looking around pointedly, 'I don't see a crowd that will make it worth my while.'

I were disappointed. It never entered my mind that I'd be refused even a look. But I could see it would be no small undertaking for the trader to shed his load. It might take him the rest of the day to get up and going again.

He were cannily studying me as all these thoughts passed plainly across my face. 'Just as a matter of interest,' he said then, 'what is it you want and how much cash do you have for buyen it?'

'I have these,' I said, holding up my rabbit skins, tied neatly in a bunch. They were alpine bunnies, all with thick creamy coats and only of a good size.

The trader straightened as much as possible and looked me over, starting with my handmade clothes that were rags before they met me and were by now hanging off me in threads. I still had the hunter's dog fur, laced around my hips, and boots cast off from the miners who grew small feet to go with their short statures. I hadn't seen my face for months, except reflected in a mountain pool, and it were bound to be grubby. My black hair was plaited into a braid and hung over my shoulder, tied with strips of leather at the top and bottom, and this is where the trader's eye came to rest.

'Comen to think of it, my throat is dry as a saltpan. Mebe I will stop for a wee while and have a cup of tea. Will you join me, girl?'

Thanking the hidden stars and thinking my luck had changed when he saw my beautiful rabbit furs, I helped the old trader off with his pack, hardly able to keep my hands off the silks and ribbons and silver bangles it were hung about with. I was forced to wait while he settled himself and got his spirit stove assembled and his water boiling. Then finally he laid out his wares on the grassy verge by the trail.

There were dresses I stroked with my roughened fingertips but had no proper use for, as well as trousers and woollens and laced leathers I did. Besides the clothing on offer there were silks and ribbons in colours I'd never seen in my life before – let alone had names to give them. Rings of silver for fingers and wrists and throats caught the light and sparkled.

I knew I looked like a bird with an eye for treasure, hopping from one jewel to the next, not knowing how to choose. A dress in blood red, embroidered with white flowers, caught my eye. The skirt fell to the knee and the bodice laced at the waist. Little Bear would leave me to my ravings if I came back to her dressed so pretty for not surviving the night, so I set it to the side. I also lingered over a blue silk scarf with a pattern of tiny leaves and mountain flowers sewn into the borders, but finally I made a pile of a pair of trousers, waxed and toughened for living outdoors, a linen shirt, a leather waistcoat and a grey woollen coat with a hood that would double for a blanket in the snow.

The old man watched me as he sipped his tea.

'How much for these?' I said, not bothering to hide my sadness at setting aside all the pretty things.

'How much do you have?' he asked me frankly.

'The skins,' I said, holding them up again.

The trader barely gave my bunnies a glance and my heart sank. It was a risk being seen and all for nothing. He weren't going to trade for my skins, and I'd already given away my betrothal, so I had nothing more to offer.

'I see,' I said. 'I'm sorry for wasting your time, old man. You can be on your way.' And I turned to leave, walking a few paces.

'Wait, girl,' the trader called. 'I know of something you can trade.'

I turned. 'And what would that be?' I asked, wary. Knowing for sure that after surviving all that time in a camp of miners with none but my wits about me, there were certain things I was never going to give away, not even for an emerald ribbon.

The trader looked me straight in the eye.

'I'll give you all of the clothing you laid out there in return for your hair.'

'My hair?' I said, disbelieving.

'Yes, girl,' he said, holding out two crooked fingers and snipping them together like scissors.

My hand went to my braid, running it through my fingers and giving it the first proper look I ever had. It were as smooth and shiny as running water and the colour of blue-black feathers.

The trader could see doubt flickering across my face. I weren't clever enough to make a show of bargaining, but he could read my reluctance as plain as the grey sky.

'Plus the blue silk scarf, and this,' he said, choosing a silver bracelet with stones set in a pattern that looked like a scatter of stars from the days before the clouding over. He held it up so it caught the light.

I weren't so innocent I couldn't see he was dazzling me, but even so I felt it were more goods than my braid were worth. I would have traded my hair just for the clothing. I needed that to get through the long nights in the high country, and besides, it would grow back given time.

'You have a deal, old man,' I said.

'Ah, good girl, good girl,' he said, 'I have scissors here somewhere.' He turned to rummage in his pack.

'No need,' I said, pulling out my knife.

The trader's eyes widened when he saw my blade and his mouth dropped open in surprise as I held my braid in one hand and with the other sliced through it at the nape of my neck.

When I held it out to him I was struck with sudden doubt.

My braid hung from my hand like a snake with its back broken.

The trader dint leave me time for thinking again, snatching the hair from my hand, lowering it carefully into a silk bag and slipping it and all his other wares into his pack quicker than I could've believed if I dint see it myself.

Before a minute had passed he was on his way, hauling his poor blinking donkey behind him, leaving me standing on the path with my pile of new clothing, blue silk scarf and strange silver bracelet sitting on top.

I waited til the trader were well out of sight down the valley then gathered up my new belongings and walked longaways back to Little Bear.

If I turned too fast my head just about flew off my neck it felt so light now, lacking the long anchor of my hair. I skipped with the pleasure of it. Stopping when I got to the treeline, I stripped off my old rags and slipped into my new clothing. The vest laced up at the front like it were made for me and the trousers, while a little long, would leave me room to grow if I had any more length in my legs to come. The coat hung about my shoulders, too warm for the middle of a bright day, but it would be a warm comfort during long cold nights. I tied the blue scarf about my head to keep the short wisps of hair off my face and last pulled the silver bracelet over my hand. I'd never had anything like it. Something pretty just for the sake of being pretty. Like the feathers of a bird, or a flower on a tree.

Little Bear lifted her head when she heard my approach but startled and scrambled to her feet before I called out to her in my old voice, which weren't changed none by my new things, and reassured her.

'Little Bear, it's just me, your old Snow, but now missing some hair.'

My bear dint care for my clothing or changed appearance and in her way told me it were getting late and time to find dinner and make camp.

For a few more days the clear warm weather kept up. I hardly needed my new coat. Little Bear and I wandered on the lower slopes around where I'd seen the trader, enjoying the mild days, then I took it into my head to go and have a look at the chateau. It had been long years since I'd seen it last and I felt comfortable now with the map of the mountain in my memory. Every day I filled in parts unknown and discovered how other parts connected together. It were time to go and see the house I'd been born in.

I took us around a ways, coming on it from above, higher up the mountain. It were a good few days of walking, but my legs were strong and my bear were willing, so why not? I was curious to see my home after all these years and there were no one to tell me not to. I weren't going to go near, just have a look at it.

Keeping to the cover of forest, I found a way to come out on a ridge where there was a good view down and across to the north.

'Stay well back,' I told my bear, who dropped to her belly and rested her chin on her paws, as if she'd decided for herself to have a nap and it were quite a coincidence I just happened to suggest it.

A field of white lay before me, notched here and there with shadow. With clouds drifting low, it were hard to make out sky from snow. There weren't a chance we'd be seen over the distance, but even so, I wanted to stay low. I peeked over the edge and I could see the chateau's high outer wall. Down the valley was the icy tomb where my father and mother and countless other former inhabitants of the chateau lay, and beyond that some way, the forest edge, where the hunter and I had run the night he'd taken me from my cell.

Without any glass to look through, I strained my eyes to see.

The chateau seemed to be in disrepair. There were places where the roof had caved in and stonework had fallen to the yard below. No smoke rose from the chimneys either, though that mayn't mean much for the stoves were usually kept burning clean. Making smoke were warmth wasted and mountain people knew better than that. Heavy falls of snow lay over everything, even in the yards.

When I was a little one there were always people crossing the main yard and using the paths around the house to tend the gardens and move animals from one pen to another. Now I couldn't see any movement at all. It looked to be deserted. After watching awhile, blinking my eyes every now and then and squinting to see better, I thought I saw a figure moving about just outside a doorway.

I lay on my front for a long time, but apart from that I dint see anyone. I thought maybe if I stayed after dark I'd see if there were any lamps lit, and that would tell me how many souls were still living there. And if my stepmother's window glowed I'd know she were there.

Just as I was considering camping right there to keep on with my watch, Little Bear stood on her back legs and sniffed the air. She were right, there was weather closing in.

We started up the slope toward the cover of forest but it was obvious even to those of us who'd been distracted by spying that the weather coming were bad and crowding in fast.

When we came out on top of the ridge we saw dark clouds piling up, coming in from the south. The storm would be nipping our heels on our path back to cover.

I felt foolish for missing all the warning signs – the unusually warm days, the still, clear air in the valley – all I'd taken for rare fine weather. Ifen I'd had my wits about me, we'd have been making our way up to one of the caves in the lee of the mountain, but we weren't going to make it there now before the storm came down on us. Instead I turned for one of the old huts I knew of, even though it were a risk. Anyone else caught out in the open would also be drawn there.

The big ice-storms seemed to be coming more often than they had in years past, I was thinking as I hurried Little Bear down the north side of the ridge, the cold descending on us as we went. It were the second storm come in since the long days started, the first being the one sent by the hidden stars that helped our escape from the miners' camp. If I were glad of that one, I were less thrilled about this one coming so close behind it. It would bail us up for days, which weren't to my liking. I felt safer when we were on the move and in the open. Now the wind were also growing fierce and I took out my she-bear fur and wore it over my new coat. There was no time for hunting dinner, so we'd be eating the dried fish and berries I carried in my pack.

The hut we reached just as the snow flurries began swirling was set back against a cliff, which gave some shelter from the wind. I pulled open the door and barred it shut behind us.

Inside it were dank and drafty, but it were built solid out of logs, the roof tied on as well as screwed in the old way and so not likely to be flung away from us into the wind. The stove had been used over the years but I dint dare light it. Not when we were likely to be snowed in for days with no way of running from anyone drawn near by the smell of smoke.

For dinner Little Bear and I gnawed on some leathered fish and sucked on snow before laying out as best we could to sleep in spite of the wind howling around us.

For the next two days I wished I were a bear soas I could have passed the time like my cub, but there's only so much sleeping a girl can do before it just won't come anymore. There was no venturing outside while the wind howled. From time to time I'd open the door for a look but when the snow piled up past halfway, there wasn't anything to see. The glass in the windows was too grimy to see through and the storm had brought such a pile of black clouds, it were almost dark all the long day. I searched the hut from rafters to floor beams but all I found was one ancient paper book.

I had books when I was a little one but none were shared with me when I was locked away so I'd lost the knack of making out letters and putting them together into words like my father had shown me. I recognised some of the shapes, the one beginning my name for starters, but most of the rest meant nothing to me now.

The book was about the stars, I could tell that from the pictures. I brought the paper as close as I could to the light from the grimy windows to make them out. It had been many years since the sky had cleared enough to see the suns beyond our own. Even the moon may have gone elsewhere since.

How were we to tell? It was like the whole earth had been wrapped in wool and put away for safe keeping. Maybe it were punishment. Like shutting a bad child in a cupboard to think on their error. The clouding over had the effect of locking in bad weather, sending it rolling around the globe, getting worse and worse before it blew itself into nothing, only to start up fiercer somewhere else.

I found the constellation that was shown on my new bracelet. There was writing about it but I couldn't make it out. The stars looked like a ship with its sail billowing out in front, crossing the black sky. What a wonder to see such a thing and only to have to wait til the dark of night.

I fell asleep looking over my book and the next I were aware, a quiet had descended outside. Inside it were still and black as the pitch of night. I couldn't see my hand in front of my face when I held it out. We'd been snowed in with even the roof covered. Why had I woken? I were warm enough in the tiny cabin with a bear and my furs, so it weren't that. I lay still and listened. Little Bear woke too, sensing something amiss.

And then I heard it, a pacing around the hut. Footsteps liken, but making hard going through the fresh fallen snow. They sounded human. Or at least they weren't deer or dog. I felt Little Bear raise her nose to sniff the air, but quiet liken. I wished she could tell me what she smelled. There were no way to tell we were inside. Our tracks to the door would be long gone and the snow stacked up past the windows, so no looking in to see us. I lay still as the dead, straining my ears to listen, but there were no more sounds. And when Little Bear put her head down to her paws it meant whatever or whoever it were had passed on.

When I woke once more it was time we got moving. I put a

spark to a rag soaked in spirit and held it up. The storm had passed over but when I pulled open the door of the hut I found a wall of snow. Little Bear roused herself and helped me dig, her thick claws and paws pullen more snow out of the way than I could. We cleared a tunnel and crawled through into cold blue light. Little Bear went first and sniffed the air before she hauled herself out. I pulled my pack behind me and swung my she-bear fur around my shoulders. The cold were already biting through the layers of my clothing.

'Come on, Little Bear,' I told her. 'We need to move or we freeze.'

There were no steps in the snow around the cabin. No sign of the human or animal that had been sniffen us out. I listened to the trees above my head but they weren't putten any messages in my head today. I set my worry aside. If they weren't worried then I had no need to be neither.

It seemed sensible to head for the caves up on the mountain where Little Bear and I had thought on going before I got waylaid by spying on the chateau. If there were more bad weather on the way, I had a mind to be out of its way and have some means of feeding ourselves and keeping warm.

It were a few days' walk and I kept us going in long loops, crossen over our own tracks. Little Bear, if she were aware, dint seem to mind the extra walking. This kept us coming back on anyone trying to follow us, but the other advantage of this manner of progressing was that I could set snares and then double back to check them after a time. And we had some luck with catching bunnies. Like us, they were digging out their snowbound burrows and looking for a meal. It were their bad luck they became ours.

Whenever we sat down in the high country we were always visited by green parrots. Unlike the hunter, I could never bring myself to wring their necks. It would have been too easy, as they walked all around, lifting their wide feet high to clear the snow, digging at my boots with their sharp beaks and climbing over my pack looking for something novel. They were just like me with my new things. I liked it when they opened their wings and I got a glimpse of the blood-red feathers underneath. It was like a secret they kept to themselves and only shared as a treat. Altogether they were too smart by a longways and made me laugh out loud with surprise at their cleverness.

A group found me and Little Bear as we set down to cook our lunch. They were happy at first with my gifting them the rabbit guts but then they came to look over the rest of my things. They made a wide berth of Little Bear after she swatted at them, claws out, but me they gave a thorough inspection.

My sleeve had fallen back from my wrist and before I could stop her, one of the parrots nipped and tugged off my new bracelet.

'Hey!' I cried. Another parrot stepped over, lifting her wings to show off her crimson feathers, and there was a tug of war over my jewellery.

I watched, helpless. I knew they weren't the kind of birds that made a treasure trove in their nests. They dint care for objects except for the fun of stealing and pulling them apart.

'Hey!' I called again, my voice breaking the hush of the forest. 'Give that back.'

Even to my own ears, trying to scold the birds into returning my property sounded foolish. So I turned away and ate my meal, figuring they would get bored before long. Watching from the corner of my eye I saw one of them, claws hooked through the chain and using the raptor blade on the end of her beak, pry open the back of the charm, breaking it in two. She seemed satisfied with her work then and, dropping it in the snow, high-stepped away to join her fellows inspecting my pack.

I walked over to retrieve my bracelet and were surprised to find a device from the old days had fallen from the charm. As I held it in my palm a tiny blue light slow-blinked up to the sky.

I gathered up the broken silver links and constellation charm and slipped them in my pocket. Wrappen the blinking part in rabbit meat, I coaxed over one of the birds and she swallowed it in one gulp.

'Come on, Little Bear, we got to be away fast now.'

I shooed the green parrots away from my pack and shouldered it. And then me and my bear were off as quick as we could through the deep snow.

I knew that bracelet was too much. Any trader worth the salt he carried dint give away gifts. And now I knew it weren't the kind I should have been grateful to get.

I were thinking it was technology from the old days. A tracker. The trader must have recognised me, taken my hair for proof, and sent me on my way with a sure means for my stepmother to catch up with me in her own time.

I worried now that my new clothing were soaked in poison, or had other trackers sewn in the seams. But I'd chosen the clothing myself. Even the blue scarf keeping my ears warm I'd set aside from a pile of others. It was the bracelet the old man had chosen to gift me.

Now it seemed likely the footsteps that woke us in the

night were human and huntsman. And the way the hut had been buried by snowfall made him walk right over us. Perhaps the signal dint work so well through six spans of fresh snow. I weren't sure as to how accurate such a thing could be. Maybe it gave a range and we could have been anywhere in it.

There weren't time to keep up our looping pattern progress, so I turned us toward a high country river. It would be a cold swim downriver and a wet hike back up but it would rub out our tracks and give us a head start. It wouldn't be long before whoever were tracken us figured out they were following a cheeky green parrot instead of a girl and a bear.

Coming out of the tree cover to a rushing river bank, I took off my pack and squashed in my boots and she-bear fur. Then, holding it in front of me for a float, I waded out in the fast-flowing stream and let it carry me away. The cold made my heart race and almost closed my throat. I had to force myself to breathe out and let my teeth chatter to make some warmth.

I knew Little Bear would follow me. She was a natural swimmer but reluctant to get her fur wet, even though all it took were a good shake before she were warm and dry again. I rolled on my back, letting the river sweep me along, not trying to go one way or another. When I judged we'd come far enough, I chose a smooth running part and started kicking over to the far bank, finding a spot to pull out where there weren't so much snow, soas our tracks weren't as easy to see. I pulled on my wet boots while I waited for my bear. I was dripping wet and already shivering enough to break a bone. I glanced into the sky and saw a falcon gliding above us. She gave a call, and two, and banked away upriver.

Little Bear found me and once she pulled out and gave her

thick brown fur an almighty shake, we took off into the forest. All I had was movement to warm my body and dry my clothing and it was a race between whether I'd get dry or die.

And it came close. The running warmed me up but my clothes were still damp, so when I was tired out from running and had to rest, the cold crept back in. It had been a while since I'd shivered so badly, the last time being back on that dark night when the hunter took me from my cell and I'd almost frozen trying to keep up with him. I were little more than a baby back then but now I should have known better.

My headlong flight had pushed me out of the coals and into the oven like Cook used to say. I needed a fire to dry myself proper but the smoke would give me away quicker than even a tracker for anyone who knew how to look or smell for it. I pressed us on, deeper into the forest, toward the base of the mountain I'd have to climb to get up to our cave. I didn't think of that right now. I was having enough trouble putting one foot in front of the other.

When my teeth stopped chattering I knew it to be a bad sign. I looked up through the treetops and glimpsed the skidding clouds overhead. And was that the falcon, back again? Swooping down now between the thick branches to give me her fierce glare? Had I turned into a mouse, crawling on the forest floor, and she were coming to scoop me up for her dinner? When I looked again she were gone.

Seeing things int a good sign. I had sense enough to know that. Little Bear started butting me with her nose.

'Stop that,' I told her, seeing now I were on my hands and knees in the snow, sinking to the wrists, and fingers turning blue. Where were my gloves? I couldn't feel the chill anymore, which were a relief. My bear pushed me again and I turned to her, annoyed.

'Leave me be!' I shouted, furious at her. And then I remembered my she-bear fur, why hadn't I got that wrapped around me? I looked around and couldn't find my pack. Had I left it? No, there it were on my back. But I couldn't find the strength or the wits to slip my arm through and slide it around.

I was lying in the snow, Little Bear digging at me with her nose, telling me to get up. But I couldn't, it were warm lying there. Maybe I was finally dry. The treetops swayed above me, though I hadn't noticed the wind come up. I felt tired all the way through. I tried to pull my bear closer, but she were being contrary and turning away. It was the easiest thing I ever did to close my eyes and slip away.

The hunter's story

»——→

'That were how I found you, girl. And when I put my hand there, your heart was as slow as I've ever felt one beating and still been inside a living person. Skin as chilled and grey as the snow you're named for. You're lucky I had more sense than to warm you up quick. Has to be a slow warming when a body gets that frozen. You been more dead than alive these past days. Lying there like a doll, barely a breath passen.

'Scared me most to death, you did. I don't ever want to see a body lying in the snow like that again, you hear me? The cold will get you out here. It's always waiting. You gotta work to keep it off, stay moving, build shelters, eat. You got to be bred for this kind of living, you can't just chance upon it. Some people have the cold deep in their bones, like maybe their ancestors survived in it. I think you got that, girl. I never met your father before he died but talk in the chateau was that he weren't made for the climate. He built the wall and hid behind it, believing the long nights would pass and the blue sky would appear again. I never heard much about your mother but likely she endured a different set of hardships. You're made from something else, seems to me. You got a toughness that goes

89

right through. Else you wouldn't have survived when I left you in the forest.

'I weren't none but a child myself then. And cocky. I hadn't yet seen the death that cold deals out. But maybe even then I saw how you stood that march through the night. Never complaining, even when your feet were frozen into blocks. Stamping your foot at me, think of it! Standing in the snow, four spans and nothing of you, speaking that way to a hunter with hatchet to hand and orders to remove your heart from your body, and still trying to tell me off. No one but you could have made it through even the first night, let alone toughed it out for years. You must have a spine of steel. Maybe I knew that somehow when I left you. It's what I been tellen myself all these years to feel better about having done it. For sure I had no choice. I had to go back to Rain with something. She had my sisters' and my mother's lives over me. It were them or you, Snow. A choice.

'For some reason you get under her skin, girl, and bother her something bad. You were growing up beautiful and strong. More than she ever would be. What difference you being around coulda made to her, I never figured out. Maybe there's something more to it than I know.

'We been here a few days now. I been getting you warmed up slow. It were a day before colour came back to your lips, turning that blood-red they are now, and all your fingers and toes saved too, thanks to me. Your bear been turning herself in circles. Growling at me coming near, like a faithful dog she is, though she should know I been only helping. Best when she just lies down next to you and gives you her heat.

'Can't believe you got that bear for a pet. She must have

given those miners a turn. Maybe they dint like her so much by the end, ifen those scars around her neck are telling the right story. And why'd you sell your hair? Such a length and you may as well have written who you were and where in the clouds for everyone to see. You been living up here by yourself too long. You need to learn something about people, afore it's too late.'

Opening my eyes were a battle. The lids were heavy and kept sliding shut the moment I lifted them. I must have been drugged.

'You int drugged. Just been close enough to death for it to follow and keep on pulling you back. Come on, time to wake up good and proper. That's it, keep up that struggle. You can make it back ifen you dig deep and try hard.'

I was lying on a stretcher by a fire glowing with warm coals. We were in one of the caves high up the mountain. Telling me off these past hours were the hunter. Claiming all the credit for saving me when it were his fault I were running in the first place. It was a shame I was still too weak to argue, and had to save up all my fury because sleep kept coming to claim me.

I heard the hunter's voice coming from close. 'Still as death you were. I might've lost you again.'

The hunter flew a falcon now. He wore a leather gauntlet on his arm where she came and sat to eat scraps of raw meat. She and Little Bear ignored one another completely, as if each were beneath the notice of the other. I admired the bird. Her fierce markings and keen eye beneath, the span of her wings when she spread them, put me in awe to see so close. After she were fed the hunter slipped a hood over her head, quick liken.

'Int that cruel?' I asked. 'To keep her hooded?'

'Cruel not to,' he answered me. 'She sees so much, putting on her hood lets her rest a time.'

I was sitting up now, the strength slowly coming back into my limbs. The cave we were camped in was dry with powdery dust under foot, rocky walls, and the ceiling covered with glowing worms when it was dark. They lit up slowly, one by one, and reminded me of the constellations in the book I'd found in the hut. Maybe that's something like how the night sky looks behind the clouding over, I thought.

I were still reluctant to leave the warmth of the fire in the mouth of the cave and the hunter kept it burning bright for I was easily chilled. His habit was to squat opposite me, resting on the balls of his feet, like he were ready to run. He wore high boots and a firearm across his back, axe at his belt. His eyes, like his bird's, darted here and there, never resting in one place for long, taking everything in. He still carried himself long-limbed and lean and the clothing he wore was different to how I remembered when he took me away from my stepmother.

I were more changed than he was. We were almost the same height now, my legs as long as his, and the gap between our ages had narrowed with the years. But he seemed more weary than when I'd last seen him, taking his leave of me in the forest that day. The lines on his face were deeper but instead of seeming hard, now they seemed forbearing. If I rested my eye on him when he was about his business, sometimes I saw a thought cross his mind that caused him pain. He'd pause in his work and bow his head, waiting for it to pass. I didn't reckon it to be an injury he carried, or a poorly healed wound, for other times he moved quick and quiet, like a wild dog.

When he looked me in the face, I fancied I could almost see the memory that plagued him.

'What happened to you since we parted?' I asked.

It were some time before the hunter began his story and it were halting when he did. But after a time he warmed to the telling.

'I took that she-bear heart back to the chateau and showed it to your stepmother, all bloody and dripping for some extra drama. She turned her nose up and bid me take it away afore it ruined her rug.

'So that were that for then. It were a hard long nights season that followed. Bone cold up there on the mountain and a cruel sickness went through the chateau, carrying off many of the children and some of the healthy adults, including my own mother. Rain came to believe the sickness were brought by the families who'd lately come in from the south. We called them Voyagers. More started coming over the high southern passes that season, saying the sea was flooding their islands and they couldn't survive there any longer. They set out in open boats and put their faith in the currents bringing them ashore on the beaches in the deep south. If they missed that landfall, there were nothing to stop them drifting all the way to the frozen seas. These are navigating people, Snow, but without the stars to steer by, they're blind.

'From the beaches in the south the Voyagers made their way over the mountains and if they survived that climb, knocked on Rain's door. She let some stay for they were willing to do the work no one else likes, emptying the latrines and clearing the ice and snow from the roofs. More'n one slipped and broke a leg. It's dangerous work, up high and in the wind.

'I went about my duties, forced to range further and further in my hunts. With the ice-storms coming in more frequent most of the game had descended to lower country and walked into the waiting traps of people needing to feed their families down there. I went as far north as the city from time to time, to see if news of you had filtered through. Ifen you'd made it to the miners' camp. I knew them to be drunkards, so it were only a matter of time before word of you slipped out. But I dint hear nothen for two seasons, and into the third.

'I wondered if maybe I'd left you to die after all. Just a wee scrap of a girl you were then with not a single idea as to how to keep from dying any number of ways. It were most likely you'd just frozen in the snow, or perhaps been eaten by dogs.

'That were a mean time in my life. With my mother passed away, my sisters were wed one by one and went away to make new lives in the lowlands. I fell into the habit of looking only to my own survival. My heart grew cold, until I were feeling little of anything and taking on all your stepmother's dirty jobs.

'After the sickness ran through the chateau, your stepmother cast out the Voyagers, shutting the gate on them in the dead of the long night, calling them the source of it.'

The hunter paused here in his telling, swallowing. 'Could be she were right but I took pity on them and guided them down the mountain as far as the main road and told them to keep walking it until they got somewhere better. That left all the work they weren't doing still to be done in the chateau and only the old and grieving to do it. Rain slung about threats and locked the pantries to get people to do her bidding. And then when this last long days season set in finally, she wanted to go to the city, saying she'd been locked up on the mountain long enough and she needed to be seen again. She made me take her there. No one else knew the way.

'Once there she looked to be outta her depth. Things had changed since she caught your father's eye and left to come up the mountain with him. Her friends weren't around anymore and she weren't up with how the people were talking or dressing. She threw tantrums and raged out of humiliation. And then one night she saw a drawing of you, Little Queen. It had sudden liken appeared all round the city. Soon it were being copied and used to sell everything from mountain water to clothing.

'In it you don't seem like you know your sketch is being made. You're looking off to the distance, hand up to shade your eyes, other one on your hip like you do, that braid you cut hanging over your shoulder. Little Bear stands at your side, and naturally people were taken by the idea of a mountain girl with a pet bear. That drawing caught the whole city's attention. People were talking about you wherever I went. Something about the look on your face and the way of your standing, it got in people's heads.

'There were no mistaken it was you and I was glad all the way through. To see you grown and living, I were relieved. But I suffered your stepmother's wrath after that. She hired thugs to punish me for not doing the job I'd been paid for. They cornered me in a dark street and turned my insides to shards of bone and pulp. Three against one, and in a tight spot. Couldn't swing my axe, and I weren't carrying my firearm. Two held me while the other broke my ribs and gave me two black eyes I couldn't see out for weeks.

'Lying there, sucking in what little air I could, I thought maybe justice had found me. I thought maybe I were finally paying the price I had due for all the bad things I done, so many I've run out of fingers and toes to count.

'It weren't to be my time just then though because people found me and recognised me as mountain folk and, Cook being known to them, took me to her. When I were half-dragged though her door, she looked at me just as she did the first day I met her. I told her you were alive, and she said she'd heard, and it were one thing I could stop blaming myself for.

'While I lay in an agony of discomfort letting my bones knit back together, Rain took that same drawing of you and slapped a reward for your return over it. She talked to the pamphlet writers, making up a sad story of how you ran away and she were heartbroken and all she wanted was for you to be back with her, your only family, safe and sound liken. I knew it to be false all the way through but she got the attention she were craving. She had a portrait drawn of her standing outside her mountain chateau, calling herself Lady Rain. Her name is Rain, right enough, but there were no lady about her I'd ever seen.

'It were after that when the city people got interested in her and she started getting invitations to parties and gatherings and such. She showed herself about, acting the part she made up in her head about being a mountain woman, though I'd never seen her willingly leave the chateau, let alone the walls, in all my time there. Still, she dressed the part in furs and feathers, and it seemed to charm the city people, if only for the novelty, and really they were laughing at her behind her back. But, after a while, it seemed she really were popular. Then I realised that the city people dint know any different. Their lives are harsh, the poor anyhow, but they have no inkling how hard life is up on the mountain. So they came to believe all the stories she made up about scaring wild dogs from her door, and bears coming to eat people in their beds.

'After a time, she ran out of money and had to go back to the chateau and to my shame I returned to her employ. She convinced some of her friends to go back with her. I brought them all reluctantly. More mouths to feed and the kind that don't pull their own weight were exactly what we dint need. We made it just before another fierce long nights set in and there were no going anywhere for a time. We were snowed in and stretched thin. It was a dark season and only the lucky ones saw the end of it.'

The hunter paused and put his hand to his side, letting out a slow breath.

'When finally the days lengthened I walked out through the gates leaving nothing behind but regrets. I went to the city to find work and found your picture still stuck up all over, but there'd been no new sightings. I thought all along it musta been one of the miners had sketched that picture of you and your bear and shared it round. No one but me knew you'd taken shelter with them, and there are mines all over the mountains up there, so any bounty hunters who set off in search of you were looking in a haystack for a needle. I thought you were safe enough still.

'There's no hunting in a city, and living costs money so I spent the long days labouring. There's plenty of work going on the seawall to stop the ocean crashing in over it every storm that comes in. It paid my way for a time and I kept an ear out for news of you. I heard it soon enough when that old trader got to town sayen he'd sold you a bracelet and you were none the wiser you were being tracked. He set up shop in the square, selling the code to those that could afford it. I went along, keeping back soas I weren't noticed. Standing at the front were a hunter by the name of Stoat I'd run across a few times.

'There's two kinds of hunting, Snow. There's stalking a deer slow and careful, studying it, creeping up, then killen it fast afore it even knows it's dead. Then the butchering is done quick and clean and all the parts useful for something. That's killen for genuine need and being thankful for it. This hunter named Stoat likes to scare his prey, corner it, put panic in its blood. He lets it see death comen. And he doesn't butcher clean. It's always a bloodbath. That kind of killen scares the hell out of me. He does his work for the thrill rather than the need.

'There weren't many could afford the code, but Stoat were one of them and that made me worry. The others were city people, saddling up on hired horses to join the fun and not likely to survive their first night in the outdoors.

'I made my own way, knowing the direction already and not wanting to be in the company of fools. Once I were clear of the city, I picked up Stoat's trail, figuring he were the one I dint want to be coming across you, and started looking for a way to prevent it. He moved quick and purposeful, on foot like me, faster than I were expecting, and it were a scramble to keep abreast of him. And then once up in the mountains, we were both of us pinned down for two days waiting for a storm to pass. Nearly froze all the way through, I did. Ifen it weren't for enough snow fallen quick to build a cave, I woulda been dead. I thought Stoat had to do the same. There were no creature larger than a grasshopper out in that weather.

'As soon as the wind dropped I sent up my falcon for a look and she let me know when Stoat were on the move again. I was close to catching up when I came across a field of green feathers. That was when he'd figured out that you fed that tracker to a parrot, and he'd taken out his rage on the birds. Dint increase my opinion of him none.

'But you slipped away right under his nose. And I wouldn't have found you either if it weren't for my bird.'

The rest of the story I knew.

Since I'd been frozen, my gaze was sluggish and slow and I couldn't imagine moving far or fast ever again. But I'd have to, and probably soon. The hunter was worried. He took to pacing between the fire and the mouth of the cave, pestering me about how were I feeling every second minute. Sayin before long we'd be cornered, pinned back against the high passes and hemmed in by bounty hunters dotted about the country below us. When he began telling me to get up and move around, forcing me to walk distances away from the fire to work my legs, I lost my temper.

'Good almighty, Hunter,' I said through clenched teeth, 'I int proud of being so weak but I can't help it. I'm doing all I can. Choosing a swim in the river were the right way to shake Stoat off my trail, are we in agreement on that?' I dint pause long enough to let him get a word in. 'I knew I wouldn't get warmed up again easy. But I also dint want to be towed back to my stepmother by someone with more stomach for cutting out hearts than you. So I thank you for warming me up but for the love of Little Bear, will you leave your nagging?'

'You need feeding up,' the hunter replied. 'Living on rabbits alone is not enough for a girl.'

So he brought me berries and wild roots, roasting them on the fire. And he found a goat with a kid by her side and hauled them back to the cave entrance where the nanny set up a racket of protest, not liken being tethered. The hunter managed to milk her a little in spite of her kicken and bleating, and fed the fatty cream to me where it sure enough did me the good we needed it to. My belly stopped feeling like it were caving in and my mind cleared.

Little Bear followed the kid with her eyes and I told her, Leave it alone. She put her head down on her paws and pretended she weren't interested after all.

I pulled out the pieces of my bracelet one evening and held them in my palm.

'Is that the tracker?' the hunter said.

'It were,' I said. 'Not anymore.'

I found that the front and back fitted together again with a click, and using my teeth, I bent the chain pieces closed where the parrot had nipped them open. I slipped it on, admiring how the stones caught the light of the fire.

The hunter eyed it warily.

'Look, it's just a bracelet,' I said, 'how it always shoulda been.'

The hunter came nearer, holding my wrist with one hand and bending close til I smelled the woodsmoke and leather I remembered from the night he tried to kill me.

'I suppose,' he granted, releasing his light hold on my hand.

We fell silent awhile, staring into the fire.

'Are we still betrothed?' I asked him.

The hunter looked surprised. 'You remember that?'

'I shouldn't have asked,' I said. 'Would I have been released if I'd forgotten my promise?'

The hunter raised his eyebrows. 'I woulda thought of a way to remind you, I think.'

'So we're to be wed?' I pressed, needing to know if he were holding me to my word.

'Not til you say so, Little Queen.'

That weren't exactly an answer.

The passes

We left the shelter of our cave before daybreak. The hunter, his falcon wheeling in the sky, my bear and me. A strange party of travellers with no consensus of direction among us.

'I want to head for the city and petition the council for my rightful inheritance,' I told the hunter. 'I'll be of age at the end of the season. I think.' In truth I weren't exactly sure how old I was.

'Your stepmother has the hills alive with bounty hunters, all after you. Ifen we leave this minute we can maybe keep ahead of them by headen for the high passes. But ifen we go toward the city we'll be walking right into their arms. Stoat int interested in anything but the reward for your heart, cut for real this time, straight outta your chest. And he probably plans on dragging you alive all the way back to your stepmother soas she can see you kild for herself.'

'We can go well west, round the great lakes, and come to the city along the coast,' I argued. 'You can find us the way, and Little Bear and me know how to travel.'

'Still,' the hunter shook his head, 'it's a risk, going any way north, even if it's west too. I'd rather get well clear over the high passes where they can't follow.'

'Why can't they follow? Ifen this Stoat person is as determined as you say, he'll just be on our tail up and over and then where'll we be? In the middle of nowhere, that's where. There's nothing on the other side, cepten more snow and forest. You said it yourself, I been up here too long already. It's time I stopped hiding and set about claiming what's mine.'

The hunter frowned when I said this, like it were something he knew to be true.

So leaving our cave in the chill before the long cloud-covered dawn, it were my opinion we put our backs to the pale light and go direct west as far as we could, keeping low and travelling fast. The hunter instead put us in the direction of south. He wanted to climb high and then follow the spine of the mountain range as it curved west, keeping out of reach of the bounty hunters who, with some luck, had less stomach for heights and cold.

The falcon were trained to call if she saw men, and with her sharp eyes looking out for us all morning we climbed higher. Once we were underway the hunter put me in the lead to set the pace. It weren't long before I felt weakness in my legs and a trembling set in. I covered it by striding all the longer but by midday I couldn't hide my weariness and we set down in the lee of a cliff for a break.

We'd been following a goat track stuck to the side of the mountain for a good while. The slope rose steeply on one side and fell away to the other, spindly clouds drifting in the valley below. The hunter had a spirit stove so he set to making us a hot meal which brought strength back into my legs. The falcon returned to her perch on the hunter's arm and he fed her for her morning's work.

'I think we'll camp here for now,' he said when I stood up. 'Won't be harm in waiting to see whether we got any tails. The bird will let us know.'

He walked a few paces to where the cliff fell away steeply and launched the falcon into the empty air. She wheeled away, climbing into the grey veil, already working for her next meal.

I scooped a bed out of the round rocks that covered the ground and, wrapped in my coat and she-bear fur, fell asleep. I stirred in the late afternoon when the hunter called to his bird and she landed on his forearm with a flurry of air, folding her speckled wings neatly away. He fed her again, and me, with warm stew from the stove. It was a draughty place to make a camp, and when the sun went down behind its cloak of clouds, the temperature fell to well below freezing. I dint object at all when the hunter lay down and put the curve of his body behind mine. Little Bear stretched out along my front and then there were no cold could touch me and I slept sound the dark night through.

I woke in the dim light of the hidden dawn. It were misty all around, the valley below lost under clouds, and above us the mountain disappearing into white. The falcon would be no use to us spotting today. Not even she could see through clouds.

The hunter's arm were flung across me, his breath in the nape of my neck. I lay still for a while, my gaze resting on the veins running beneath the skin at his wrist and his pulse beating slow. When he woke, he were on his feet in seconds and we packed quick. Stirring Little Bear with a prod, we went on our way, following the path one step at a time, the water vapour opening for us and closing behind. The hunter led, with the falcon on his arm. The stiffness in my legs told me yesterday had been good for them. I were gaining back my strength, and I kept up with the hunter's long strides, which put me in mind of the night in the snow long ago when reaching for his steps were as far as I could stretch my small legs.

No doubt the hunter owed me a debt, in a way. Leaving me in the middle of a forest, just a child as I was, weren't kind. And then accepting my offer of marriage, when it were never his intention to kill me anyway, could be called something less than honest. And then along with that, now holding me to it. A promise made by a child too young to know her own mind, and in a desperate fix no less. He had saved my life when he found me freezing in the snow just now but I dint feel inclined to count that against his debt because if he hadn't been chasing me along with Stoat, I wouldn't have been risking my life on river crossings to get away. But on the other hand, I were glad it were him who found me.

There weren't as much clear-cut about right and wrong as I'd once believed there to be. If the hunter hadn't kild the she-bear I might be dead now. And I wouldn't have survived the night without her fur. It seemed to me that every action set off a spinning wheel of possibilities. It made me dizzy to try and think them through.

Walking through clouds makes a person wet. Little by little those clouds soaked through the layers of fur and wool I were wrapped in and the damp chilled my bones. Every now and again Little Bear would pause in her following and give herself a mighty shake, drops of water spraying off her thick brown fur in all directions. I were used to standing clear when she did this but the hunter was caught unaware and took most of what dampness Little Bear cleared from her fur on his own leathers.

He growled at her to take herself away if she were going to shake all over. Little Bear paid no mind at all. She were not concerned with the hunter or his comfort. I fancied she dint mind creating these difficulties for him. She'd been too young at the time to remember the killen of her mother, but all the same she seemed to harbour some suspicion toward my future husband. Perhaps in her bear mind she knew my fate and thought me a fool for it. There were no explaining the complicated workings of humans to a bear.

It were a difficult few days of walking, with cold camps that were endured rather than welcomed. Climbing was hard and by the end of the day I longed to rest my legs. But after the cold of the night, in the morning I were eager to get walking again. So in this way days and nights went on from one another. The hunter not being one for light conversation, I dint often try to engage him, and I were used to long silences from my bear, so after a time I stopped thinking. My mind went as blank as a beast's as my legs covered ground.

The hunter chose high goat paths that tended due west. Once or twice we came upon a herd of those tough-hoofed creatures and made one our dinner. To catch it, we bade Little Bear hang back downwind soas she dint spook the herd and I chose one to get around in front of and drive back to the hunter. They were light on their feet, especially the big ones, rarely setting a foot wrong on the steep slippery ground, but easily outwitted and caught, not being used to seeing people. They made delicious eating. The hunter showed me how to cut up the carcass quick and efficient. Which parts were the best eating, which ones to give to Little Bear and the falcon, which not to.

The hunter became convinced we'd left the bounty hunters behind.

'There int profit in following this far,' he said. 'Cost them more in time and effort than it be worth in the end.'

'Than I be worth, you mean,' I corrected.

'You be worth more'n any sum writ up on a poster, no matter how many zeros it got behind it,' the hunter replied, catching my eye and holden it longer than I were used to.

'You trying to remind me of something?' I asked. 'Because I haven't forgotten. I never will, unless you tell me I can.'

The hunter couldn't hold my eye then and looked away, turning back to the trail.

I felt bad. I dint mean to go hurting his feelings.

There came a day when the hunter's falcon cried out her alarm. He stopped and looked to her, listening. She called the alarm again, two close cries, different to the ones she made to her own kind. These were the ones she were trained to make.

'It's Stoat,' the hunter said. 'We been going too slow.'

I weren't sure how we could have been going any faster but a party of three will always be slower than a man on his own with a reward on his mind. There was nothing we could do but carry on, following the goat trails, staying up on the high ridges. It were looking like we'd be walking through the night, dangerous as it was. We daren't stop and wait for the bounty hunter to find us in our sleep.

The clouds descended on us once again as the diffuse light of day began to fade. It were cold and getting colder when we came around a corner and found ourselves on the edge of a deep ravine. Stepping perilous close to the edge, the hunter peered over and told us there was a rushing river at the bottom. I could hear it, white water tumbling over itself to fit through the narrow gorge. To our left hung a sagging swing bridge, still attached by both ends but showing no promise as to how long it would stay that way. Once it had been a solid construction of high tension rope, wire and boards, but now it were a fraying, rusted, almost-broken thread stretched across a chasm.

'We can cross and cut it down behind us,' the hunter said.

'Little Bear won't go,' I told him. 'She has more sense than to risk her neck on that contraption. And I won't leave her behind.'

The hunter pressed his palm to his forehead in frustration. 'Can you see another way across this ravine, Little Queen?' he said.

He only called me that when he were in a mean mood.

I made a show of looking, just to save my pride.

'She'll follow you, if you lead,' the hunter told me, kinder now. 'It'll mean the end of being chased.'

He was right about that. One way or the other, the end would be quick.

I turned to Little Bear. She were sitting on her haunches in the way she had of telling me, No way. I put my hands on my hips in my way of telling her, It's happening whetheren you like it or not. My bear turned her ears back and put her chin to her chest, showing me the top of her thick skull.

'Stubborn as a donkey, you are, Little Bear,' I told her. 'This is the only way. Now are you coming, or not? There int no longaways round this time.'

My bear put her nose in the air and yawned, showen us all her teeth, then stood up and, reluctant liken, followed me toward the swing bridge.

I caught the hunter's eye as we passed and he shook his head. 'I said it, but I dint think you really could make her do it.'

I had to be first out on the precarious contraption if Little Bear were going to follow, so I were the one to test its strength by placing a foot and then joining it with the other. I held the hand ropes tightly and went slow, one step at a time. It weren't so bad as I thought. The boards were slippery with rain and slime and never being used, but they held my weight. Little Bear didn't have hands to help hold her balance so she spread her legs wisely and kept three wide paws in contact with the boards at all times. I glanced behind. The hunter was staying on the firm ground.

'I'll follow once you're across,' he called.

It weren't possible to look behind and in front at the same time so I set my mind to the crossing, talking calmly to my bear all the while.

It were taking an age, even to get to the middle. The further we left solid ground behind, the more the void of empty air filled my mind and fear bloomed like a dark flower. Now we could clearly hear the raging waters of the river below, and the bridge rocked beneath our feet, caught in the wind blowing through the tunnel of the ravine.

'Halfway there, Little Bear,' I told her. 'Keep going.'

I had to tell her this for she'd stopped moving. A stronger gust had swung the bridge to the side and just as I'd bent my knees to absorb the movement, Little Bear had put her belly to the boards to hold on. Now she was having trouble getting up the nerve to get going again. If my instincts were anything like her animal ones, they were saying to get low and cling on, nevermind what happens after that. But I knew we had to keep going. There weren't no rescue and nowhere else to go except a plunge to a watery grave.

'Come on, Little Bear,' I called to her softly, half turning so she could hear my voice. 'Up you get. We're almost there.'

But to my horror there was no shifting her. I took a couple more steps, hoping to draw her on by leaving, but she were still flat on her belly, clinging to the boards, her long claws gouging the slime and muck on the bridge.

I glanced back to the hunter. He had one foot on the crossing, like he thought he could come and give Little Bear a kick in the backside to get her up and moving. I waved him back. The weight of an almost-grown bear and a girl were one thing. Any more and we'd all be in the river sooner than we could take a breath.

And just then the falcon landed on the hand rope above Little Bear's head and started up a raucous squawking. She flapped her wings around my bear's head like a furious dishmaid until Little Bear got her feet underneath her and started inching forward once again.

The falcon dint finish her work there, instead swooping and nagging at my bear until we safely set foot on the other side, then she banked away, easily escaping Little Bear's claws as she rose on her hind legs to take a swipe at the bird.

The hunter made his way across steadily after us, hand over hand. A few metres from our side he had a scare when one of the boards fell away under his step. He caught his descent with an elbow wrapped around the rope rail and my heart pounded painfully. But he were as surefooted as the mountain goats, and with a hop and a jump he were by my side once again.

I wrapped my arms around him. Seeing him safe I realised I could breathe again.

He held me tight. 'We made it,' he said simply. 'I dint think we would.'

And with no time lost, for the bounty hunter appeared just then on the other side of the ravine. It were too far to see his expression proper but it was safe to assume he weren't pleased. He set a foot on the bridge to begin his crossing but thought better of it when the hunter and I both set to work, him with his axe and me with my knife, sawing through the fraying rope bindings on our side.

Instead, Stoat took to a knee and reached for his crossbow, aiming it at us across the chasm.

The wind tunnel was working in our favour now and his first shots were wide. By the time he'd adjusted his sights, the bridge was falling away and we took cover along the trail. Cutting the bridge were an act of vandalism I weren't proud of but I were also not sorry to leave the bounty hunter behind.

We turned back to the trail and after a time my nerves settled with the walking.

'How'd you make your bird do that? Pestering Little Bear into getting off her belly?'

'I dint do it,' the hunter said, turning to look at me. 'I thought it was your animal-whispering.'

I raised my eyebrows. 'I don't know anything about that,' I said.

'Girl, I think you know more'n you let on, more'n half the time.'

The dance

‹———≪

We were descending toward the lake district in the west. The air grew warmer and instead of wearing our furs, we took to carrying them across our backs. In the middle of one afternoon, with the walking to warm me, I took off my coat and rolled up my sleeves. It were a glorious feeling to have fresh air on my skin. The hunter did likewise with something like a spring in his step. His shoulders weren't so set and he gripped his axe lightly.

It was easy walking in the lowland country and we covered ground faster than we ever had before. The falcon kept a lookout, her cries carrying through the clear air, but none were alerts. The hunter made long strides and there were a pleasure in placing my feet in his footprints, though I had to put in a little skip every few steps to match them. He glanced behind and raised an eyebrow.

'This int a square dance, Little Queen.'

But he were smiling, at least with one side of his mouth.

Lowland country turned to forest and we picked our way west along deer paths, choosing this one then that one in the general direction we wanted to go. The trees stood close enough to whisper to one another but what I heard dint sound familiar. Were it possible trees in different forests spoke to each other in foreign tongues?

I asked the hunter.

'You hear the trees speaking to one another?' he said, stopping to look at me.

'Don't you?' I said, surprised.

The hunter raised his eyebrows in answer, looking at me like I'd lost my mind.

'It int speaking exactly,' I said. 'More a kind of whispering.'

'You hear trees whispering to each other?'

'It int like a person were whispering to me. I don't hear it through my ears liken. It's more like a thought I get that they're passing on to me.'

'You hear the thoughts of trees? What are these ones sayen?'

'I can't understand these ones. That's why I asked you about whether trees have different languages,' I said.

'You're an odd one, Snow, that's for sure. People don't usually hear trees talking to one another. You've spent too much time alone out here.'

That much were true and there were no denying it.

Nearing dusk we came upon a path showing human footprints in the mud. We followed it a ways cautiously and when we came to the forest edge we saw glowing lights coming from the windows of a town. I could hear music carried softly on the breeze.

'It's a bar,' the hunter said. And then seeing my eyes light up, 'We can't be going anywhere near. Don't even be thinking it.'

On this I weren't taking no for an answer.

'We certainly are,' I replied. 'You said yourself just today that I've spent too much time in the forest alone. I need some social skills and right there is the chance to make a start on them.'

I bade Little Bear stay put. She turned a few circles, making herself a bed of pine needles, and settled down with no arguing – unlike the hunter, who grabbed my arm, telling me it wasn't safe to go among people. I shook off his grip and instead caught his hand, pulling him along behind me.

I'd never felt more sure about anything in my life than I was about hearing that music up close for myself. I set off toward the sound. By the time we got near the music were almost as loud as it would be inside, and my heart were full. I pushed open a heavy wooden door and the scene inside took my breath away.

It were a big room with a bar along one wall and tables pushed to the sides. Warm light spilled from spirit lanterns hanging around the ceiling above the heads of a group of musicians playing an array of instruments I'd never in my life seen before. A woman stood singing, dark hair like mine pulled over one shoulder, and warm olive skin gleaming with sweat. Her voice was rich and full and she clapped her hands and stamped her foot in time with the music.

As I stood in the doorway, the hunter closing out the cold night air behind us, the tempo started to grow faster and my feet longed to fly away with it. I pulled off my muddy boots, passed my coat and furs to the hunter and joined the dancers, closing my eyes and letting myself be carried away. The music was happy and sad at the same time, the words in a different language but it dint matter for they carried the feeling with them strong and true.

The hunter edged his way through the crowd, holding my things, and leaned on the bar, ordering a drink which he sipped at, eyes scanning the room. His gaze rested on me from time to time and I liked him watching me. The music flooded my senses and filled my heart. I copied the way the other dancers were moving but mostly I kept my eyes closed for it seemed the best way to let the music flow right through my skin.

I was forced to open my eyes when a stranger caught my hand and I felt his other on my waist. If I should have been more worried, I couldn't find it in me to be because my partner knew the steps and it were no effort at all to follow him in them. I whirled around until I were too dizzy and laughing to think straight.

The stranger wore a shirt open at the neck with light pants that I could tell had sat a horse but had not been lived in like mine. His shoes too were light, as if they were made for dancing. What kind of person owns shoes specially for dancing? I wondered. I danced in my bare feet, soft from being inside my boots, the boards of the floor smooth and cool under my heels. When I grew hot I unlaced my vest and threw it to the side, letting the cool air touch my skin. I felt I could dance for the rest of my days. There was no end to the joy of the music.

Too soon I were forced to stop, or look like a fool, for the band took a break. Resting their fingers from flying over keys and strings, they went to the bar and wet their dry throats with ale. I was left looking into the face of my partner. We were almost of a height, him with dark hair recently cut and a clipped moustache above his top lip. He took a step back and bowed. I weren't sure what to do with myself and could already see the hunter elbowing his way past people and coming toward us.

'It's my pleasure to make your acquaintance, Little Queen,' the stranger said.

For certain I wasn't sure how, with my hair cut short, but he'd recognised me.

I stood mute. My social skills being what they were, I could think of nothing to say.

The hunter came to my side. 'What do you want?' he said. 'She int for sale for no price.'

'You're right, Hunter. There int money enough to buy this kind of beauty.'

The hunter rolled his eyes, which were plain rude.

'Forgive my intrusion,' the stranger continued, 'but I wanted to meet the girl in the picture that has become so famous.' Turning to me he said, 'You must have quite a story to tell, Little Queen.'

'That int my name,' I said, my voice sounding rough to my own ears.

'My apologies,' he said, bowing once again.

I was getting a little tired of all the bowing.

'Stop that,' I said, harsher than I meant to, and he straightened, eyeing me.

'My name is Snow. And I'm just a girl. There int anything queen about me. I'm pleased to meet you,' I added.

The stranger raised an eyebrow toward his snipped-close curls and his moustache twitched. Was he laughing at me?

Reaching into a pocket in his pants he drew out a card. There were words written on it that I couldn't read. I looked up in confusion. What was I meant to do with it?

Too late I realised he saw I couldn't read the writing. My spine stiffened in shame.

Smiling smoothly, he said, 'My name is Fox,' and held out his hand.

It were ignored by the hunter and I both. The hunter took the card from my fingers and glanced at it. He made a tsk sound with his tongue and flicked it to the floor. Then he shoved my boots and coat at me and pulled me toward the door.

Already thinking me ignorant, I dint want to be taken for rude as well.

'Thank you for the dance, Mister Fox, but we must be leaving,' I said over my shoulder.

'You're welcome, Snow. I hope our paths cross again one day,' he called after me.

It broke my heart to leave the dancing behind, but I knew it were best. 'You were right,' I said to the hunter. 'I'm not ready for socialising.'

In answer he caught my hand and brought it to his lips.

'You got more queen in you than you let on, Snow,' he said.

The back of my hand burned from his kiss. I shook him off.

'You're laughing at me, just like that stranger. He could tell I've forgotten how to read. I'm just a mountain girl.'

'I'd believe you, Snow. I really would – if I hadn't just seen you dancing.'

The music stayed in my head the rest of the night. I would have paid a high price to go back to that dance every evening for all my living days. But I'd been recognised, and it was lucky Fox were just a strange nut and not after the reward. If I dint want to get us all in a mess of trouble, we had to stay clear of bars and dancing.

'Do you know what all those instruments were called?' I asked the hunter.

He admitted to knowing a few and so I questioned him late into the night until he was so sick of me he pretended to be sleeping.

I was too excited to sleep. I'd have been full of surprise if I ever slept again.

The dairy

>>-------->

Villages and towns began to appear now and then on our path. We always went the longaways round, hunting for our own dinner, though sometimes we could smell the roasting meats and baking bread coming from farm kitchens. It had been so long since I'd tasted fresh bread I begged the hunter go and knock on a door to get me a loaf. He refused, sayen it would attract attention our way.

We came across livestock more and more often. Mostly cows who were easily spooked by Little Bear and would stampede across a field in panic if we passed too close. That meant a farmer would lift his head from his work and wonder at what was drying up his milk, so we had to go wider. Even chickens set up a cackling and a squawking if my bear were up wind. It got me thinking, what were we going to do with Little Bear in the city? She couldn't very well just trot along behind me through the business district, could she? I asked the hunter.

'This only entering your mind just now?' the hunter said in answer.

'Well, give me leave for being slow on the uptake, but I've no idea what a city looks like let alone how it behaves.'

The hunter raised an eyebrow as he always did when my tone got haughty.

'Don't worry, I thought of that. I have friends and we can leave your bear in a barn for a few days while you get your business attended to.'

'She won't like that much,' I said, thinking aloud.

'She's done much more'n that for you on being asked. I have it in mind you'll convince her somehow.'

And then the city was only a day's walk away.

Under cover of an evening sky, the hunter led us to a farmhouse in the last range of hills afore we came to the coast. When he knocked on the door a round woman and the smell of baking bread greeted us.

'It int you? I don't believe my own eyes!' she said in surprise and pulled the hunter into a hug. 'Come in, come in, afore the chill creeps in. You're in a world of trouble, my boy.'

I was left standing on the step, unsure of whether my bear were invited and thinking probably not. It were a long while since I'd stepped foot in a household but I knew that wild bears are not usually invited to dinner.

And then the woman's gaze fell on me. 'Good lord of mercy above the clouds, it's the Little Queen.'

'My name is Snow,' I said, offering my hand. 'And this is my bear,' I continued, standing aside.

The woman's eyes widened until I thought her eyeballs would fall out.

'Now, now, Noelly, don't be making a fuss,' the hunter said, pulling me inside and waving Little Bear in after me. 'It int as crazy as it looks.' He shut the door fast behind us. 'The bear is tame.'

Little Bear confirmed this by walking through the cottage to the kitchen, where she found a warm stove and settled herself down in front of it like an oversized dog.

'I can't believe I'm saying it but the bear being tame is the least surprising thing about you knocking on my door. There's folks out all over looking for this girl. Her picture is up on everything. There's mad interest in finding her.' Noelly took a strand of my hair in her fingers. 'Such a shame you cut it, girl. What a rope it were. Now on display in the great gallery, by the way.'

'That can't be right—' I started, but the hunter cut me off.

'That's enough of that talk, Noelly. She's just a girl and she's been living up in those mountains her whole life. A prisoner, then a slave, and now running for her life. She knows nothing about any of that carrying on.'

'Hunter, holy mother of Maggie, how'd she end up with you?'

The hunter shifted his weight. 'That's a long story. And some I'm not proud of—'

'We're betrothed,' I said, surprising myself.

Noelly raised both her eyebrows and then shook her head slowly side to side. 'This int the kinda conversation to have standing in the hallway,' she said. 'Let's sit and eat.'

Noelly shared her house with a number of cats. They pushed against our legs and napped on high shelves and came and went from the kitchen as we talked. Grey and black and tabby and ginger, I'd never seen so many of the slinky creatures in one place before. 'They keep down the rats,' Noelly told us. 'And their conversation is considerable more intelligent than any I'm likely to find hereabouts.'

Meeting the wide green gaze of a fluffy white cat that had jumped on my lap, I were inclined to believe her.

Our host's ancestors had been farming her acres as far back as anyone could remember. Since before the floods and the clouding over. Then there used to be a thousand beasts on the property, but now she kept it to a few dozen. Without power it weren't possible to keep more than that many milked. She and her hands did that themselves and the milk were picked up by wagon and taken to the city daily. It were a life of early risings to frozen mornings, year round. Though the cows dried up in the long nights, it were just a matter of waiting until the turn, Noelly said, then the milk came back, provided not too many had frozen to death where they stood, of course. She were always looking for what to put by for those times. Never quite enough wood to burn or food to store. Her years of labour showed in the creases on her face, but along with the lines made by worrying, there were plenty there from laughing, which she did a lot.

During the evening she shared her home-brewed beer with us and her laugh lines got used more and more.

'I don't go to the city much these days,' she told us. 'There int anything much there for an old woman like me. Less of course I took it into my head to go looking for another husband, I suppose!' she slapped her hand on her knee and laughed.

The hunter smiled politely and I grinned because Noelly's laugh were infectious even when you dint get the joke. 'What happened to your last husband?' I asked.

'He dug himself a hole and when he fell in it he dint have the sense to dig himself out again,' Noelly told me, folding her arms across her chest.

I weren't sure what she meant. The hunter smiled and shook his head, setting his eyes on the floor. I was missing something but I had no idea what.

'So you live here by yourself then?' I asked, thinking it were a struggle to be in company and my skills were sorely lacking.

'True enough, girl, except for my cows and cats and whatever else is hanging about pestering me for a meal. Present company excepted, of course,' she finished, swigging the last of her beer. 'It's always nice to have visitors that talk back when addressed directly.'

This was also funny, apparently. I felt like I were walking through conversational quicksand, and sinking more than I were stayen afloat.

'Can the bear stay here while we do our business in the city?' the hunter asked while I was thinking of my next line of polite enquiry.

'So long as she doesn't spook my cows, she's welcome. I dare say they'll get used to her in time. She looks to be tamer than most of my cats,' Noelly said, glancing toward Little Bear, who'd laid herself out by the fire on her back, her paws in the air. 'You sure she's a wild animal?'

I went over and rubbed Little Bear's belly, settling down next her. The rug was deep and warm and dry and I was full of food and as well as all that, making conversation with a stranger had worn me out. I let my eyes close and drifted off to the sounds of the hunter and Noelly talking quietly.

'How old she be, Hunter? She int old enough to wed. And neither are you, if it comes to that.'

'She's older than she looks. She gave me her betrothal to save her life when she was a child. But I was never set on killen her. Now it's a joke between us. I tease her with it, that's all.'

This I heard as if I were listening at the end of a long tunnel.

The hunter dint want to wed me? He thought me a child and was playing along. But it hadn't seemed that way when he'd caught my hand and kissed it after the dance. Or saved my life when I'd frozen in the snow. Or by the way he looked at me sometimes when he thought I weren't aware.

'I got to clear my name,' I heard the hunter say quietly.

Noelly muttered something back but I dint catch it over my bear's snores. And then they turned their talk to an even softer pitch and I was drifting off to sleep.

The city

»————→

The city was a shock to every one of my senses. I was dazzled by sights and deafened by noise. I had to cover my nose from the rotten stink that crept in and made my mouth taste as foul as a tainted river. And it came on quick.

We set out first thing and soon the farmhouses started coming closer and closer together til there weren't any space between them, neighbours sharing a house but for a wall between them. The dirt roads turned to paved, and my heels tapped on the hard surface with a jolt that carried up to my hips.

No wonder city folk get worn down so quick, I thought, walking as they do their whole lives on stone streets.

The city proper was behind a great wall, built to shelter those within from the pounding sea on one side, and the ice-storms and gales that blew in from other directions. The wall was as thick as a man is tall, and higher on some sides than others. It weren't built for defending from the top, just for strength and to shelter behind. So it was not in any way beautiful, being constructed from any and all scrounged materials. I made out old vehicle tyres and lengths of rusty wire held together with a mix of pounded earth and water, left to harden. The hunter told me it was being worked on all the time, this part being shored up after the last big gale, this part being strengthened against the relentless wash of the ocean. The wall couldn't stop snow from falling on the city within, but that dint happen much, he said, being close to the sea as it was.

As we passed through one of the gates into the city proper it were falling to dusk. The hunter had timed it that way so we could put our hoods up against both the cold and being overly noticed. Noelly had given me the disguise I wore. She'd done some adjustments quick to one of her old dresses she said she wore when she were a newlywed. Yellow with tiny white flowers, it fitted me fine except in the bust where I evidently weren't as filled out as Noelly had been upon her marriage. I insisted on keeping my old trousers on underneath. It were only sensible. And I laced my leathers over the bodice of the dress. Noelly said this took me back to looking like myself and shook her head, her efforts wasted. I had looked to the hunter and he just raised his shoulders like he dint have an opinion either way. So we settled on me wearing my coat over all of it and keeping my hair tucked up under a scarf, which Noelly showed me how to tie just so. The hunter rolled my furs tight, hiding the she-bear, and we pushed this to the bottom of my pack. It were the long days season so we could do without furs and look more like city folk and less like we'd climbed fresh off the mountain.

Little Bear got the idea we were leaving and stirred herself from her comfortable rest in front of Noelly's stove. The hunter nodded his head toward her and I knew it were time. So I knelt in front of my bear and whispered the plan to her, that she couldn't come to the city with us, it weren't no place for bears, especially tame ones, so she had to stay right here with Noelly and the cats and wait for me to come back to her.

It weren't that she were understanding what I was saying, language being no use to a bear, it were more that she read my expressions. And not just those I made with my face but also how I held my chin and probably even what I smelled like. The words I spoke were for me. When I finished she expressed her objections as she always does, yawning widely to show me all her teeth and turning her ears back. But finally she nudged me with her wide dry nose, telling me she understood. I hugged her around the neck though I knew I shouldn't, she weren't a person, but I did it for me, to say goodbye.

When I looked up Noelly were shaking her head slowly side to side, looking to the hunter as if to say she couldn't believe her eyes.

It weren't anything he hadn't seen before.

The hunter led us through the streets as people lit spirit lamps, setting up tables for trading at a night market. There was clothing and dry foods and stews and soups and breads ready for eating. Of cakes and sweets I'd never seen the like. Piled up like sugared mountains they were.

'How are there enough people to buy them all?' I asked the hunter, but he shushed me and bade me turn my gaze to where I were placing my feet for I'd tripped on a gutter once again. I were as used to uneven terrain as a goat but for some reason the flat paving kept catching me by surprise. The hunter caught my hand and pulled me along fast, both to keep me on my feet and to pass a man opening a violin case and tuning his strings.

'No time for that. We need to get to a safe place to sleep.'

But just then I were forced to dig in my heels because we came upon a stall in the market that took my breath away. On it were arranged cups and plates stacked neatly one on the other, plus bunting strung out behind and posters pinned up, all bearing my face and my bear's. In some I were portrayed as the hunter had once described, gazing up and away with a faraway look and Little Bear at my side. I took it immediately for Bushy Beard's work. He'd captured my likeness in a moment I weren't aware he were looking. And he'd drawn me not in the usual cruel way he showed his fellow miners but like I were grown tall and knowing my own mind. My braid hung over one shoulder and I recognised every part of me except my clothing had been changed from the rags I wore every day at the camp, to a dress of blood red with a bodice of blue embroidered with white flowers, with the shawl I wore now wrapped across my chest. It were exactly the dress I wanted to buy from the trader that day on the mountain.

My mouth fell open as I took in my face on all of the wares. Some posters showed me being cross at the hunter leaving me in the forest. How'd anyone known about that? I wondered. It looked just as I'd remembered it, except my clothes weren't the same and there were imagined details like bunnies watching from the bushes and unlikely looking mushrooms sprouting up through the snow. I were drawn glaring at the hunter, fierce and scared, my hands on my hips. The word I took to be 'Reward' were written underneath with a number so large it must have been a mistake.

On a plate resting on a stand all its own was the portrait my stepmother had made me sit for. I were a child, sitting on a fancy chair, kicking my heels and wearing a scowl. In the front was Rain, dressed in finery I had no memory of from that day, including a golden sash worn from her right shoulder across to her hip. It looked to represent an official office of some kind.

I dint have time to look closer, for the hunter grabbed me now around the waist and pulled me away. 'Put your head down, Snow, for the love of Little Bear. Do you want to be mobbed and torn limb from limb?'

The rest of the short walk were a blur to me and I let the hunter almost carry me along, I was so stunned by what I'd seen. Finally we came to a door right on the street and it opened quickly when the hunter knocked. He shoved me inside with a hand in my back.

Throwing off my hood I turned to face him, furious. 'Hunter, you better tell me right now what you been keeping from me these long months because what I saw out there makes no sense to me at all.'

'You know all there is to know, girl,' he answered, back to being mean for no reason I could see. 'It int anything I can explain. Doesn't seem like commonsense to me but yours is the face everyone in this town wants to see on their plates and spoons looken at them of a morning.'

He shrugged his shoulders and slung his coat over the back of a chair, setting his firearm next to it. Sitting himself down, he pulled off his boots and put his feet before the fire, not at all ashamed of the holes in his socks.

I looked about me. If it were an inn, we were the only guests to be seen and it weren't a surprise, for the plaster was crumbling from the walls and there were a gritty layer on the floor I could feel through my boots. Still, the fire were warm and it being the only way the room were lit, anything worse to report on the standard of our accommodation lurked in dark corners.

The boy who'd answered the door was still staring at me but he tore his gaze away when the hunter asked for dinner for us both and paid him, making it clear that the money weren't for the quality of the meal he was expecting, but soas our presence weren't advertised.

I sat next to the hunter by the fire with a heavy sigh.

'Why did Noelly say you were in a world of trouble?'

'Me being with you. She thinks it will bring me strife.'

I weren't convinced about this for Noelly had made her statement before she'd even seen me and my bear standing on her doorstep.

'Why is my stepmother wearing a golden sash across her shoulders on that plate?'

'She's married to the mayor now,' the hunter answered simply. 'She's the first lady mayoress.'

'When were you thinking of sharing this information with me?' I was furious.

'I only heard it from Noelly last night. I dint tell you soas you would come quietly into town and not draw attention to yourself with your temper.'

I was both offended the hunter judged me ill-tempered and cross he was right.

'What hope is there then, of getting back my mountain?' I said. 'If she has the mayor's ear, my story won't even get a hearing.'

I couldn't believe it. Everywhere I went, my stepmother were there before me, spoiling and ruining. 'All I want is what's rightfully mine,' I told the hunter.

'Right now we need to lie low. I have some friends in the city and we might be able to find a way.'

'Find a way?' I said in despair. 'It shouldn't be a matter of finding a way. My claim is good and true. The mountain is mine. Left to me by my father and held in trust by her until I'm of age. All I need is to get before a judge to hear my case. Int that right?'

'I know that, Snow,' the hunter said, patient liken. 'But you're wanted as a runaway. She'll lock you up again as quick as look at you. She's still your legal guardian.' He picked up my hand now but I shook him off.

'I know you think me a child,' I told him. 'But I know my own mind.'

It were a long and restless night spent thinking on my troubles. I were shown to my own room where I lay in the dark, trying not to wonder about the creatures skittering about on the floor below me, and instead feeling cross at myself and the hunter in equal measures. He was keeping things from me, I was sure of that, but I hadn't a clue what they were. My stepmother were now the first lady mayoress of the city and she'd been spreading her lies about me being a runaway for all these years. Playing at being the bereaved mother just wanting her child back and even offering a reward higher than it made sense to. Ifen I even stepped out on the street without my hood up I'd be recognised and taken to her whether I were willing or not. And she was still my legal guardian.

Added to my troubles, I weren't exactly sure when the day of my birth fell. The precise counting of days were not a specialty on the mountain and without a real mother or father to care about noting such a day, I'd lost count of all but the number of seasons past.

The mountain custom was to mark a person's temple with ink under the skin at the end of each long night's season. It were a way of celebrating survival but also an easy proof of age. But I were shut away in my cell before I reached the first mark of ten seasons, younger children being too young to stand for being pricked, as well as too likely to die for age to be worth noting. After my father passed away there was no one to count for me. By the time I'd come to the miners, I'd never been marked and no one cared enough to start.

Our run from Stoat and the other bounty hunters had brought us near to the end of the long days. Soon the chill would turn bitter and the sun would hardly rise behind the cloud cover before it sank again. Instead of feeling safe and dry with a roof over my head, I started to feel those four walls pressing in on me.

Cook's story

Only when pale whispers of daylight started creeping under the curtains did I fall asleep. I woke still weary and in a foul temper and went searching for the kitchen to ask for something warm to rouse me. Looking into the hunter's room I found him long gone.

He's left me, I thought. Left me shut up, as usual, in a cell, in a hut, in a cave, an inn. Passing time waiting for the next thing to happen to me. I was sick of waiting and hiding.

Going into the kitchen, I knew a fraction of a second before she turned that the woman standing over the stove were as familiar to me as the face of my bear, though it had been a long time since I set eyes on her.

'Cook!' I cried and ran across the room to fall into her arms. I couldn't believe I was now taller than her by half a head. My last memory was wrapping my arms around her middle. Now I were the one bending into the embrace.

The years had been hard on my old friend. Once a rounded figure, I could now see Cook's shoulder bones through her clothing and there were shadows in her face that told of times she'd been hungry.

'Snow, my girl. It's so good to see your face,' she said.

She bade me sit at the solid table in the middle of the room and brought me tea and eggs for my breakfast, sitting down near me. I held her hand in mine, my eggs steaming and tears filling my eyes.

'Nobody's cooked me eggs since you did the last time,' I told her.

'Now, now, dry your tears. I'm here now and both of us better off for it. Eat your breakfast and we'll talk over it.'

I turned to my plate and scooped the eggs obediently. Once they hit my belly I felt my bad mood lifting.

'Tell me where you been and what's happened since I last saw you,' I told her as I mopped my egg yolk with fresh-baked bread crust.

'Oh, it be a long road that brought me here. It'll be a long telling.'

'I got time,' I said, grumpily.

Cook raised her eyebrows. 'The long of it to short, I'm here now. I came down the mountain with Rain and were in her employ until she found her new husband. Then when she moved into her fancy house, she had no need for a mountain cook more used to serving up rations than fashionable dinners, so I were let go. Up the mountain I had more than a full day's work every day feeding hungry mouths and stretching out what had already been extended beyond reasonable. Here I'm cooken a few meals a day with hardly a shortage of ingredients and nothing to trouble my conscience.

'But more than that,' she said, sighing and pressing a hand to her belly, 'we'd all been living with Rain for so long, it'd become habit to stay quiet and keep the peace, for everyone's

134

sake. When I realised I were starting to believe her lies, I were glad to go, or be left with no self-respect at all. You were long disappeared, the hunter gone too, so there were no strong ties to take me back up the mountain. Shame on me, I couldn't face another long nights up there. That last one one nearly kild us all. And getten worse every year. I never want to feel the likes of that cold again.'

Cook paused and I saw her hands curled into fists in her lap. She knocked away a tear that had fallen to her cheek and set her face again.

'So there int anyone living up there now?'

Cook shook her head. 'Rain left without a backward look. The turbines were broken down by then and no animals left in the yards. The last storm we had broke what was left of the window glass, letting in the snow. There be no one but cats and rats running the halls there now.'

'I saw the roofs are caving in,' I told her.

Cook nodded sadly. 'It were a grand house in the old days but not well suited to these times.'

Then it were time to tell my story.

So I told how the hunter left me in the snow with none but a knife to my name and how I got my bear and ended up living with the miners those long years while I grew and then how it all turned sour, with them chaining up Little Bear and us having to run. And how I'd been tricked and tracked then frozen in my flight and found by the hunter.

'Who were one of the ones doing the chasing, mind you,' I said, as I were still sore on this point. Then I told her how we travelled far to the west, still being hunted, and to Noelly's dairy and finally ended up right here.

'Noelly's my sister,' said Cook. 'Getting odd in the head with only her cats and cows for company, I hear.'

Remembering our ramshackle conversation, I were inclined to agree but too polite to do so out loud.

'So if Rain is married again and settled in the city, she has no need of my father's mountain anymore.' This dawned on me slowly. 'She's no reason not to give it back to me if she doesn't want to live there.'

'You're right she don't want to live up there, Snow. But even so she won't be giving up the mountain. It has a value in dollar terms as well as being part of her whole First Lady Mayoress Rain image she's put up all over. That be three too many titles she's awarded herself in my opinion, but there you go. She shares the bed of the most powerful man in the city and if anyone knows what she's capable of, it's you. You best be careful how you play your hand for she'll lock you up again and it won't be me able to deliver you a knife this time.'

So I had to settle my mind once again on keeping quiet and waiting for word from the hunter.

For the next few days he left early with his hood up and returned late, shutting himself away from me in his room between times and saying nothing of his doings. My pride prevented me asking. After all our hard travels together it seemed unbelievable we were at odds now, but he were keeping things from me, and I still held onto my grudge at him mistaking me for a child.

Also playing on my mind, over and over, were the conversation I'd overheard before the fire at Noelly's. The hunter were pretending to keep me to my betrothal but he really thought me too young and too silly to wed. It weren't like I'd ever had my heart set on him, but my feelings were hurt.

Still, I missed him. I'd grown used to placing my feet in his footsteps as we travelled snowy paths. And I were cold every night without him lying behind me in the way we'd passed our nights on the road. How could it have come to this?

I longed for the comfort of my bear. She were like my missing shadow. I was constantly turning around a full circle, looking for her, before I remembered she was left with the cows and the cats on the dairy.

Most mornings I rose and helped Cook in the kitchen, staying out of sight of the inn's few guests. I washed and dried the dishes and put them away. While we worked I told Cook with pride about how I'd remembered what I'd seen in the chateau kitchen and worked out how to cook and clean for the miners. She shook her head and laughed when I told her of my many mistakes.

The kitchen were warm and dry and caught the morning light and so when the breakfast was served and cleaned up, I sat at the table and watched Cook as she made the day's bread. Sometimes there were pamphlets to read. Small boys came to knock at the door, selling them for cents. It were the way most people got their news. While Cook kneaded the bread she helped me run over my letters once again and I practised my reading on the news sheets. It weren't long before I remembered what had been lost and was reading without hardly moving my lips.

But I was almost sorry I bothered some days when the pamphlets brought news of my stepmother.

Mayoress Visits Voyagers' Camp

First Lady Mayoress Rain stepped out yesterday to visit the North River Voyagers' camp. She wore an elegant dress of plain cream wool with beaded details at the collar and hem, perfectly suited to the solemn task.

She spent the morning passing out masks to protect against the spread of disease, wearing one herself that had been made to match her dress. Speaking to correspondents after the event she expressed her concern for the plight of the Voyagers and her gratitude to those assisting in the efforts to set up the camp on the edge of the city.

'Soon there will be stalls selling everything they could ask for,' she said. However she also emphasised the importance of keeping a tight check on the security of the camp, saying, 'Until every one of the Voyagers has been issued with identification papers, it isn't safe for them to enter the main city.'

Asked if she'd heard any news of her own missing daughter from the Voyagers as they'd travelled over the mountains, First Lady Mayoress Rain was forced to shift her face mask to wipe away tears. 'Still no clues as to her whereabouts,' she managed to say.

I rolled my eyes. As if the woman had a tear to spare for me. Probably crying because her feet were frozen from being outdoors for once in her life. And safe for who? I wondered. The Voyagers or the city people? What did a piece of paper with a name on it prove? And if they weren't allowed to leave the camp to find work, how were they going to buy everything they could ask for? It made no sense. I picked up another pamphlet.

Council Approves Increase in Height of City Wall

Late last night a new round of funding was approved for the staged increase in height of the outer city seawall. Experts continue to monitor the raised ocean levels.

'Each season free tidal flows continue to rise,' said one expert observer. 'It's only a matter of time before the pack ice breaches the seawall. Once this happens, the general consensus is that the ice will be forced into the city main, causing untold damage.'

The new spending will be funded by an increase in municipal rates, the council minutes report. The only dissenting vote came from Councillor Fox, who as usual registered his opposition to further spending and was loudly booed in chambers when outlining his alternative strategy of relocating the city further inland.

Fox were the same name as the man who'd danced with me at the inn. I remembered his dark curls and wry smile, the way he'd called me Little Queen with a twist in his lips and claimed to have sought me out of curiosity. It were plain then, if I'd known about city ways, that he were dressed fancy enough to be a councillor. The pants he'd worn had not seen hard riding, and I remembered the shoes he wore were specially for dancing.

I told Cook about the dancing and she laughed at me.

'There was no fun such as that at the chateau, that be for sure,' she said as she wiped a baking tin dry with a cloth. 'I'm glad for you, Snow.'

'Cook,' I said, a thought striking me, 'do you remember the day and month of my birth? I just were thinking, you might be the only person who has a recollection. Were you working in the kitchen when I was born?'

It seemed to take Cook a long while to stack the tin in the cupboard. She turned it round and set some others neat before she finally pressed her hands to her knees and stood up.

'Snow, it's time I told you a story I heard. And you'd best stay sitting because it's going to be all new to you. This happened a long time ago, after the clouding over, but before the cold really set in. Times were kinder on the mountain then. Not easy, mind you. It were never an easy life up there, but afore the seasons shifted to what they are now. Crops grew and could be put by for the winters, and there were still pastures for stock.

'I was just a girl, working in the kitchen under the cook before me, doing the dishes and bringing in the firewood, but I had ears all the same. The old cook used to gossip with the kitchen staff and they said your mother couldn't carry a child to full term. Over the years she'd lost one after another and with each loss the life seemed to drain from her. She weren't strong to begin with, being brought up the mountain from the city by your father, and after years of suffering the loss of babies, soon she were as pale and wispy as a ghost.

'More'n once I were frightened half to death at the sight of her unexpected as I came into a room. She could sit so quiet and still, and who knows, maybe she were part gone along with her babies. It were common knowledge that despite her grief she still longed for a child but many in the kitchen were of the opinion she should leave her husband's bed and stop putting herself through the pain.

'Then one day there turned up at the gates the first Voyagers to come over the passes seeking refuge. Your father invited them around his fire and they told him about their long journey by open boat, following the currents until they hit our shores. Their islands had been flooded by the sea, salting their fields until the people went hungry. We dint have a language in common so they told their stories in snatches and mainly by acting it out to make themselves understood. We weren't to know then but things were going to get a lot worse for those poor souls over time.

'There were a young girl among them, dark of hair and eye, heavy with a child about to come and no family with her. Perhaps they'd sent her away ahead, or somesuch. It weren't clear how she'd come to be on her own in such a state. The others stayed clear of her, as if she carried a contagion rather than a baby. It was born while they were with us and in breach. I remember hearing her screams all through the house. We did all we could for her but she was small and weak from the boat journey and the hard walk and soon after the baby was born the girl died from the loss of blood.

'None of the other Voyagers would take the child. They made clear it were tainted in some way. Your father was saddened to hear it but he weren't one to judge the beliefs of others. And it wasn't long after that when the Voyagers moved on. They were looking for land they could farm and left in search of a place to make a new life. They took all their possessions on their backs except for one they said dint belong to them. And that were you.

'It brought roses back to your mother's cheeks to have a baby in her arms, but she only had the joy of you for a few days before a fever took hold and burned through her. Others in the chateau fell ill but only your father's wife, wan as she were, passed away.

'Women's lives on the mountain tend toward short and hard, Snow. And you have suffered more'n many for that. Losing one mother is a tragedy but losing two is a grievous start for any child. For all that it never set you back. You were always looking for the next fight to get yourself into. The only sign of your misfortune was that temper. Being told what to do and how never sat well with you. I should know for I were often the one charged with looking out for you when you were toddling. The number of times I were in trouble for not doing my work because I were too busy getting after you, I couldn't count.

'So there you are. It int so different to what you been told. That poor girl who bore you left no trace of her people. Your father dint feel you were any different to a child of his blood and never thought the truth worth the telling. He loved you like you were his own, so where's the difference? And he couldn't predict what was to come, though maybe he should have had a clue after he wed Rain and came to see something of her true character.

'The knife you carry now, the one I gave you, belonged to your mother. The one that birthed you. It were just about buried with her, but I held it back at the last moment.'

My hand went to my knife. It were true the bone handle were different to any I'd seen. And the markings were not the letters that were becoming familiar to me again now.

'I remember riders coming to the chateau soon before the hunter took me away. What do you know of them, Cook?'

Cook frowned and tilted her head to the side. 'I'd forgotten all about those men. They were asken after you, I know that much. They were looking for a child born of a Voyager. I dint tell them anything of what little I knew. Without knowen their intention, it were best to hold my tongue and that's what I told everyone to do. It must've rattled Rain though, because she sent for the hunter to do her dirty work once the riders were back on the road.'

'They knew who my real people are?'

'Could be,' Cook said. 'But also could be that who they are don't work in your favour, Snow. You can't go leapen to any conclusions. Besides, a baby born to Voyagers could be anyone.'

'And what about my coming of age?'

Cook looked to her fingers and counted on them. 'Your birth fell at the end of what used to be called summer. It being none but a poor joke to call it such now. By my reckoning, when the dark only lasts a four-hour night this season, you'll be passing the sixteenth year since that sorrowful night you were born.'

I pressed my friend's hand and kissed her cheek. There were nothing more to say just then. I took the stairs to the roof and sat under the clouding over to think it through.

Cook's story changed nothing and changed everything.

Hearing boots in the street below I leaned over and saw two men. By his height and bearing, one was the hunter, though his hood left his face in shadow. The other was shorter and stubbier and held out something for the hunter to take. He did so, quick liken, slipping his hand to his pocket. It could have been notes of the money the people used in the city, or papers of some kind, folded small.

The men parted, the hunter entering the front door of the inn and the stubby man walking away along the street. It weren't a miner I knew, for I could recognise all of them better than I ever cared to, but there was something in the set of his shoulders that brought memories of those men to mind.

At the end of a week I found the hunter and Cook talking quietly together at the kitchen table. When I came in the hunter and I looked into each other's faces for the first time since we'd arrived. His look were guarded as always and I couldn't read what went on behind his eyes, but what I thought I saw was pity. My temper flared.

'What news, Hunter?' I asked cold.

'Cook's been telling me the story of your birth.'

I sat heavily in a chair opposite him. 'What of it?'

'There's no written record of your father's will. It's your word against hers he left you the mountain and your position weaker now we know you're not his true-born heir. Doubtless your stepmother knows that already and is holding it back til she needs it. Considering her position I'd say that's an end to the matter. You have to leave the city,' he finished.

None of his speech were to my liking.

'And live where, Hunter? In a cave? Slitten the throats of goats to live on and freezing to death one frostbite at a time? No. It's not the life I want.'

I'd made him angry. His eyes hardened and the scar on his cheek turned white.

'What *do* you want, Little Queen? To be waited on like your stepmother? To issue orders no matter the consequence and make others feel less than they are?'

'I'm nothing like her!' I said, standing up all the better to raise my voice. 'You said you'd help me and instead you sneak around doing deals with miners in the shadows. Are you selling me now? Back to those trolls?'

'What have I done to offend you?' the hunter said, his voice quiet again. 'I saved you more'n once in your short life, why would I now be setting out to sell you?'

'You've killed me as many times as you've saved me, Hunter. And I don't need you to do either anymore,' I said, taking myself by surprise. 'You're the one who should go back to the mountain.'

With this our eyes met, something like pain flickering across his face before it quickly turned to resignation.

'As you wish, Little Queen,' he said, bending his head toward me and mocking me with the name.

Cook put out her hand and caught his wrist but the hunter rose from his seat nevertheless. Picking up his firearm and pack, he slung both over his shoulder and let himself out the kitchen door quietly and with not a single backward glance.

'Why is he being like that?' I said in disbelief, sinking down to sit and pressing my hands into the scratched table top. 'Why is he giving up so easy and bidding me back to the wild? I can't live forever on my own, Cook. I want a life, not just surviving. What am I going to do?'

'I don't know, Snow. But now it be down to you.'

Rain

———⋘———

I needed my bear. I left Cook's house under cover of the late afternoon dullness and walked to Noelly's farmhouse. When I came in her kitchen door Little Bear bowled me over and, with front paws on my shoulders, pinned me to the floor to lick my face all over.

'Good almighty!' Noelly said in alarm, for she thought the bear were biting my face off. Then she said it again in astonishment.

When, after some time, I managed to push Little Bear off and sit up, I thanked Noelly for looking after her and asked for a bed for the rest of the night. I hardly slept then for thinking and, my nerves getting the better of me, we were up again before the light to make full use of the short day.

Saying our goodbyes to Noelly and the cats, we walked down the road, the cows not even looking up from their grazing, they were so used to the presence of a bear among them now. Just outside the city we left the road and went into the forest a ways. Here I changed out of Noelly's old dress and back into my mountain clothes, lacing my leathers and pulling on my boots. My hair were long enough now to plait into a short braid, and the day were cold enough that when I swung my she-bear fur around my shoulders it dint seem likely I'd overheat.

'Stay close by,' I told my bear. 'You're not going to like the smells too much, but you get used to them.'

And this is the way my bear and I entered the city once again. This time wide out in the open.

'Let them see us,' I told my bear. 'This time I'm Snow and no hiding it.'

I held my head high and kept a firm grip on Little Bear's scruff. I could tell she were feeling flighty among all the people, more'n she'd ever seen together in her short life. Her heart might have been racing, just like mine, but she kept her nose down and stayed close to my side. As we approached the market lanes, people were startled and cried out at seeing a wild bear walking by. I tightened my grip on her fur and murmured softly til she calmed down.

'There int nothing to fear,' I told her. And, Hold your nerve, girl, I told myself.

I heard whispering coming to me on the breeze.

It can't be! That's the Little Queen, I swear.

In my life, I never thought I'd see such a thing.

A wild bear! Walking tame as can be!

And then, louder as I came closer to the square, *It's the Little Queen. It's the Little Queen and her bear!*

But no one dared to come close and grab me for my stepmother's reward. Just as I thought, having Little Bear at my side put a stop to that.

The path before us cleared, people dropping their tasks and looking up to gaze at us with naked wonder. Some pulled their children closer on sight of my bear. And some left their business and followed us at a safe distance. By the time we reached the square there was a solid crowd of people behind us, forgetting their astonishment and beginning to chatter among themselves.

My heart leapt. What were I thinking? How would my plan ever work? I were nothing but a mountain girl. What did I know of city laws and legislations? How were I to know how to claim what's mine? But I couldn't rest easy until I'd put my side of the story. There'd been enough lies and falsifications spread about by my stepmother and I were blasting sick with it.

I reached the steps of the council building in the middle of the square.

Hawkers and beggars, usually sitting there for scant pickings, cleared the way until I had no choice but to mount the steps, pulling Little Bear beside me. I looked up at the bright brass doors of the council chamber, gleaming in the morning light. They were shut fast, seemingly against me and my bear alone. My will failed at the thought of pushing them open. What if they were locked during the day? I were so naive I never thought it through. Of course it were folly to imagine I could just walk into council and have my case heard, just as I felt like.

I halted before the doors, my thoughts all in a tumble.

'Little Queen! Little Queen!'

'First Lady Mayoress Rain is desperate to see you again.'

'There's a reward for your safe return, did you know?'

'Little Queen, where have you been all these years?'

The calls came from the crowd behind me. I could hear the jostling and murmurings of speculation.

Children called out to my bear, 'Little Bear, Little Bear, show us your teeth!' before collapsing in piles of giggles and being shushed.

I came to a decision and, lifting my chin, I turned to face the people of the city.

'I will answer your questions,' I called out, hoping my voice would carry across the square. 'I will make my case in the hope that fairness and commonsense wins over greed and self-interest.' But then I was at a loss. Where to start?

'My name is Snow. My mother died soon after my birth and my father some years after that. Before he died, he told me the mountain would be mine when I came of age, held in trust by my stepmother until that time arrived. She is the woman you call First Lady Mayoress Rain. When he was gone she turned my home into hers, making the people who had always lived there work for her. When I dint behave as she liked, she shut me in a room for three seasons until she grew fearful of my growing up and claiming back what was rightfully mine, and bade her hunter take me into the forest and bring back only my warm bloody heart.

'This the hunter could not do, and instead he set me free to make my own way if I could. The next years were hard and cold and full of thankless labour in a miners' camp. Still I was not free. When my stepmother offered a reward for my capture I had to run again and almost died being chased by the men out to claim her money. By going the long ways round, I made it to the city. And here I stand now. I am coming of age and I claim back my mountain, in front of you all. My stepmother does not care for it or love it as I do. It's where my people are buried and it's my home.'

I paused and there was silence from the crowd. I waited. Would they believe my story and support my claim, whatever good that would do? Or would they turn on me and believe Rain's story over mine?

Behind me I felt rather than heard the gleaming brass doors open with a soft gush of cool air from the chamber beyond. Turning slowly, with my hand to Little Bear's scruff, I saw my stepmother in the grand doorway. It were the first time I'd seen her since I pushed her down the stairs that day long ago when I were hot with temper, but there was no mistaking her. She were more regal now, dressed in dripping gold finery, her hair lighter, but still shining and piled on her head in an elaborate style. On her arm was a man made to look smaller by his wife's grandeur but nevertheless unmistakable as the mayor of the city, dressed as he was in the robes of the office. A long cloak of deep scarlet trimmed with feathers I recognised from high country birds were draped around his shoulders and he wore a chain of heavy brass around his chest.

But it weren't the mayor who addressed the gathered crowd, it were my stepmother, leaving the arm of her husband and coming to me with open arms in a cold embrace that barely touched me. I drew back in alarm and Little Bear raised her lips in a snarl. Rain turned to the crowd.

'As you all know I have searched long and with a broken heart to find my stepdaughter who went missing long ago in the forest near my mountain home. A small child, confused and mourning her father as we all were, she ran away to escape nothing worse than a loving stepmother and a comfortable home. After that there was never a trace of her found, until recently, when she was discovered to be alive and living in a miners' camp, now a grown girl. When I reached out to welcome her back to civilisation, she fled, taking to the wilderness once again. We can only wonder why she was hiding. What wickedness has she committed that she didn't want anyone to learn of? How did she earn her keep there? Her run from me then involved damage to council property and the considerable expense of a high country search.

'Good people, I know you have followed this story closely and I'm sorry my stepdaughter has not turned out to be the girl you had hoped she would be. She is just a runaway who has avoided doing her duty to her family. She must answer the charges of damage and wasted resources, regardless of how I feel. It would be wrong of me to use my position as first lady in a demonstration of favouritism toward her.'

Rain looked at me, showing the crowd her expression of sorrow mixed with concern, neither of which I believed to be genuine.

With this speech, which sounded like it had already been written in the pamphlets that found their way into kitchens across the city, she turned and disappeared into the gloom of the chamber, never giving me, supposedly her long-lost stepdaughter, another glance.

Council guards appeared and took a firm hold of my arms. Two more approached my bear from behind and shot her with a dart before throwing a weighted net over her. Before she had time to react, the sedative took effect and Little Bear fell to the ground. They gathered the net and dragged her into a large cart that had been driven into the square.

It all happened quickly, and I'm not proud to admit that when my bear was shot, I lost my senses and started screaming and kicking at my captors.

'No!' I cried, trying to go to my bear, though I was held fast. 'None of this has to do with her. Let her go!'

In some dim corner of my mind I knew I was giving Rain exactly what she wanted. I could sense, as I lost my temper, the crowd backing away from me. If I behaved like a wild animal they would believe her version of events. She'd planted the seed of doubt in their minds and, seeing me kicking and screaming, they began to wonder whether they could believe my story after all.

So I stopped my struggling. I placed my feet on the ground and lifted my head. The guards wouldn't set me free, but they loosened their grip and, as I was led away, I called out in a clear voice, 'I need to see Fox. Tell him to come.'

Gaol

I were shut away again. This time in a gaol cell with a low bed and a high window. My pack and furs were taken away, along with my knife. I was left with just my coat and a thin blanket. I shivered through the night with no visitors except those that scuttled across the floor or rustled in the ceiling. Even sleeping in the outdoors were warmer than being enclosed by those four damp stone walls.

Through that long night I worried over what I'd done and longed for my bear. And not just her huge furry warmth. Yet again I were the cause of her confusion and pain. I cursed myself and vowed over and over that if I escaped this, I would never again put her freedom at risk. Mine I did not worry about. At that moment, I felt I deserved to be shut away.

What put it into my head that I could walk into my stepmother's town and have my case heard in fairness? I were nothing but a stupid mountain girl. If only I'd stayed up there in my camp, keeping out of the ways of city folk, my bear safe and free.

But even as I wished it different, I knew all I'd done were in an effort to make myself a life that weren't just about hunting down my next meal and finding a place to sleep where I wouldn't freeze to death before morning. I dint know how to have a life worth living, but I knew that hand to mouth weren't the way. I had to try something different. And the beginning of that something different would be getting my mountain and my father's house back.

The seasons were long and hard, I knew that already, but from when I were a child I'd known every part of that chateau and how it worked. If I could get back there I'd get some animals and make the turbines run again. I'd repair the roofs any way I could, even if it meant doing it myself. There were still good mountain people, clinging onto a life up there, and if we worked together I were sure we could repair what my stepmother's neglect had ruined.

My father, not being of the mountain himself, had not really known how to run the place. He'd relied on the wisdom of others and those had died off or left one by one. The chateau crumbled and the outhouses rotted in the damp. My fingers itched to nail and patch and grease and sweep away the cobwebs and dust of the years I'd been away. So the more I thought about it, the more I saw that my only regret was involving my bear in my troubles. I should have left her on the dairy with the cows and the cats.

My eyes were gritty and stinging when wisps of dawn showed through the window above my head. I sat up and tidied myself, smoothing my hair and braiding it. I straightened my crumpled clothes as best I could and waited. Whatever the day brought, I would face it. I would find a way through this for my bear, no matter what it cost me.

It weren't too long before there came a rattle of keys at my door and the bolt slid back. Just as I'd requested, it were Fox who appeared in the frame. He looked every part the city councillor now. The road clothes he'd worn when we met were replaced by those crisp and clean sort owned by those who could afford them. He approached where I stood and took both my hands in his, stepping close to me, familiar, like we were when we danced together. I dint take a step back, instead holding my ground as his face came close to mine.

'Little Queen,' he began, his lips showing white teeth underneath his neat moustache. 'What were you thinking? Why didn't you come to me for advice before announcing yourself on the steps of council?'

'My bear,' I said. 'Where is she?'

Fox frowned. 'Taken to a sanctuary. She is quite well. Don't worry yourself on her part.'

'Is she shut behind bars?' I persisted. 'Because if she is then she can't be well.'

'There are fences, yes, but she has wide grounds to roam. She is safe and well cared for, don't worry.'

As long as there was wire between Little Bear and open territory, I knew she weren't happy and neither were I.

'You need to put aside concern for your bear, now,' Fox went on. 'We need to prepare for your trial. You won't be able to help your bear from the confines of the city gaol and that is where you're headed if your stepmother has her way.'

I pressed my lips together and tried to gather my thoughts. The sleepless night had scattered my wits to the winds. I was at a loss as to how to collect them back. Fox pressed my hands with his smooth soft fingers. It felt reassuring.

'Let's get you a warm bath and breakfast for a start,' he said.

'I'm allowed to leave?'

'I've paid your bail. A considerable sum, but I am a man of means and luckily for us your stepmother is not aware of our acquaintance.'

Fox led me from my cold night's accommodation, through the complex of cells, and out a door to a laneway and two waiting men. They walked one in front and one behind us along the quiet city streets, eyes alert and hands close to their weapons. Lifting his hood and saying I should do likewise, Fox kept his eyes to the ground.

I were grateful for the fresh air, though it were bitingly cold, and also glad to see Fox had retrieved my pack and furs from the bailiff and one of his men carried them now. In this way we moved swiftly. I refused the arm Fox offered. Having travelled over mountains on my own two feet, I weren't in need of assistance with walking a city street. Putting one foot in front of the other came as naturally to me as breathing in and out. No matter how cold I were, or how weary, or how worried, placing my boots on the ground had always brought comfort, and I took that comfort now as ahead of me lay uncertainty and disquiet.

After a time we came to a high iron gate that were opened for us swiftly on greased hinges. Entering the hall of a grand house, there were people to meet us. My boots were pulled off and my coat removed and soon we were warming our toes and fingers by a fire in one of the front rooms. It was the fanciest room I'd ever seen. Brocaded furniture sat on plush rugs and heavy textured drapes hung from the windows. All about me were jewel colours, deep blues and teals and the darkest crimsons and sea greens. A fixture hung with clear crystals was suspended from the ceiling and Fox caught me puzzling over how the spirit lamps were lit at such a height. He chuckled at my wonder and I snapped shut my mouth and vowed to stop embarrassing myself by being impressed. All the furniture and finery were nothing compared to drops of morning dew caught in a spider web, or the delicate suspension of icicles from the branch of a tree. I weren't going to be moved by the kind of beauty money could buy.

Bowls of delicately spiced porridge poured over with thin cream were brought to us and I ate standing before the fire. Fox sat on the edge of a sofa, watching me with an eyebrow raised as if he were waiting for the next way I would reveal my thoughts. I finished my breakfast without further comment and as I did it seemed the house woke up. I heard more footsteps outside in the hall and bells rang faintly in other parts. The sound of drapes being slid back on their rods came to me from nearby rooms. There was a knock at the door and one of the men who'd accompanied us from the gaol entered the room and spoke quietly to Fox.

'I'm afraid I'm called away, Little Queen. My work intrudes upon our breakfast.'

He stood to leave.

'Wait,' I cried. 'What happens now?'

'We prepare to defend you in court. The charges have been laid.'

'But what about my claim to my father's property? When will that be heard?'

'You've been arrested, Snow, you must understand. If you are found guilty you will go to gaol. First things first, you have to escape that fate, then we can attend to the matter of your father's estate.'

'What am I charged with?' I wondered aloud, stunned.

'Falsifying your own death, harlotry and vandalism. The charges of animal cruelty and being a runaway were dropped at the final moment from lack of material evidence.'

'None of those are true!' I cried, incredulous. 'I were kidnapped, assaulted and hunted. And I never hurt an animal in my whole life and never would. I always kill quick and clean.'

'As you say, Little Queen. And we'll gather the evidence to prove it. I apologise, but I must leave you now.'

The trial

»———→

In the weeks that followed I were taken to the city court daily
and made to stand and listen to the lies being told about me.
The court room was grandly appointed with plaster scrolls
atop pillars and gold-leaf paint on the walls. Three judges sat
at a high bench, wigged and robed, so that I could tell one from
the other not at all. It seemed they changed seats daily, just to
confuse me. In the middle of the court at two wide desks sat
Fox and his barristers and, opposite, the mayor's prosecutors,
likewise disguised under wigs and gowns soas to be not quite
like men but instead daunting instruments of the law. At the
back was the public gallery. On the first day of the trial these
pews were packed.

I stood tall in the defendant's box and glared at any who
would meet my eye, no matter if they were friend or not. I
insisted on wearing my own clothing, against the advice of my
counsellors, and braided my hair and wore even my furs indoors
because I felt this to be true to myself and my mountain. As
time passed and the public gallery slowly emptied, I realised
too late that I had misjudged. I shouldn't have appeared before
them dressed in a bear fur like a mountain savage. I would

have made a better impression dressed the part of an innocent girl in order to sway sympathies my way. But even if I could have persuaded my conscience to make me this allowance, by the time I grasped it, it were too late to change, and there were no one left in the public pews to notice anyway.

Fox and his learned friends argued my case against the mayor's office but hard evidence in my favour were scarce. My stepmother had gathered experts and physical evidence of my crimes. One officer presented pictures and testified on the damage done to the high country swing bridge the hunter and I had cut to get away from the bounty hunter Stoat.

This were one charge I couldn't deny outright. It were true we'd cut the bridge down and a shame it were, I agreed. Rain claimed Stoat were really called Officer Stoat and he weren't a bounty hunter at all and instead he was trying to rescue me from the hunter. It were him she'd put in charge of what she called the 'expensive high country search and rescue party' sent out to bring me home safely.

So it was her word against mine that Stoat was trying to harm us. I could present no evidence of him firing on us across the gorge, only my word, which came to nothing in this court of men and wigs and robes. The judges frowned upon the damage to council property.

'Call on the hunter to tell our side of the story under oath,' I told Fox. 'He were there and fired upon just as I were.'

'Even if we could find your hunter, which we cannot, he would be arrested immediately. He's wanted for murder.'

'Murder?' I cried. 'But he never kild me, only undertook to.'

'Not you, Little Queen. Another matter,' Fox said.

And then the miner I'd named Surly appeared against me,

claiming that I sold myself in return for my room and food. He tendered as evidence the scraps of underclothing I'd worn as a small girl and then grown out of and discarded. Displayed as they were pinned up on boards they looked ragged and shameful but in themselves were evidence of nothing at all. Fox argued the same and questioned the character of the miner, reading from a statement by his wife speaking of his hard drinking and poor attention to his dependants.

'It says here, sir,' Fox read, 'that the mother of your two children saw you but twice in a span of four years. And she received a few dollars from you at each occasion but only after she had confronted you in the bar you'd found your way to and demanded you hand over what was left in your pockets. Which by then were none but coins.'

'Well, leastaways I dint poison a whole blasting river just to get at one girl, as some might have.'

Fox blinked in surprise at the sudden change in the direction of his cross-examination. He were nothing but quick on his feet though and he grasped the implications of the miner Surly's accusation at once.

'What do you mean by that statement, sir? Who poisoned a whole river? And by *girl*, do you refer to the defendant who stands before you?'

But Surly grasped he'd said too much and pressed his lips together to prevent his tongue getting him further into trouble.

Fox didn't ask more about the poison, but he affected a slow walk back and forth, the tips of his fingers pressed together as if deep in thought. He then took another significant pause to write some notes, holding the court's attention while he did so, deliberate liken. By the time he'd finished with Surly, to my relief, the judges seemed to be of a mind to discard his evidence against me.

The next charges were those of falsifying my own death. On these my stepmother herself gave evidence. Standing in the witness box across the court from me, the first lady mayoress held herself regal and dignified. A small crowd had gathered in the gallery and she performed for their benefit, acting heartbroken and betrayed, draped in furs and silks soas to soften her sharp edges. It were her testimony that summed up the case against me. She described the she-bear heart that the hunter had brought her and the blood-stained rug was unrolled on the court room floor with a dramatic flourish. But instead of it being her that ordered my heart cut out, it was the hunter and I who had set out to deceive her. Which, I was horrified to realise, we really had.

Fox chose not to cross-examine Rain, telling me it were only likely to bring to light the time I pushed her down stairs, which I'd told him about, and wouldn't endear me to the judges presiding. But he did call Cook, whose kind face lent me strength as I stood in the box before the court.

'It was your understanding that on the night in question Rain ordered the hunter to take Snow from the chateau and return with evidence he had murdered her?' he said to her.

'That's correct, sir,' Cook said, nodding.

'Thank you, madam. No further questions, your honours,' Fox said, sitting down.

The prosecutor stood and approached the witness box. 'But you didn't actually hear the mayoress give the order, did you,

Cook?' he pressed. 'You were simply told by the hunter that those were his orders, and we've already established that he was conspiring to falsify the defendant's death.'

'That weren't how it went,' insisted Cook.

'Nevertheless,' the prosecutor said, flicking his robes out behind him and taking his seat.

And soon after Cook's evidence the trial was over.

The judges stood and shuffled out of court to confer among themselves and decide on the truth of the case brought against me.

My legs felt weak and when I turned my head it was light and loose on my neck. I fell to my knees and Fox's cart was called to take us back his grand house. From a far corner of my mind I watched as I was half-carried into the house and put on my bed. I drew my knees up to my chest and, turning my head from the light of the day, slept.

I dreamed of being back on the high passes once again, pursued through a thick fog. The clouds closed in around me and they were a material thing, pressing on my chest soas I could barely breathe. Sometimes I were chased by the hunter and sometimes it were Stoat.

After a time I became aware of Fox sitting by me. He held my hand and looked into my face. I could see his lips moving but I couldn't untangle the words he spoke. They seemed to trip over one another and end up all in a jumble. I had the impression of the meaning but not the detail. As he talked I slowly understood that the verdict had been brought. He was explaining the sentence the judges had imposed.

'Do you understand me, Snow? You are to remain free. They

have dismissed the charges of harlotry but found you guilty of vandalism and falsifying your death. But you will not go to gaol. Your sentence has been suspended.'

'What does that mean?' I murmured, struggling to capture the meaning of the slippery words.

'You will not go to gaol,' he repeated. 'But there are conditions.'

'What are they?'

'You are exiled. You must cross the mountains and leave forever. Never come back.'

Leave my mountain? Cross the passes to the south? 'Can I take my bear?'

'No, Snow. Your bear is being rehabilitated. She'll be released to the wild when she's deemed skilled enough to survive by herself.'

I bent my head and tears fell into my lap.

'There's another way,' he said. 'A way to stay here in the city. The court will grant you leave.'

And then, instead of sitting in the chair beside my bed, Fox knelt and asked me to wed him. He held both my hands in his own, his eyes on my face, looking for an answer.

I was in Fox's debt, both pecuniary for the bail he'd paid, and also for my legal representation. I weren't so naive I didn't know that. I had no means to pay him and no hope of claiming my property while I were under indictment.

'If you're wed to me the court would grant you leave to stay in the city, under house arrest for a time, but nevertheless comfortable and safe,' Fox said.

He'd negotiated the deal. He'd bought my freedom.

He slipped a ring on my finger that held a gem such as I'd

never seen before. It flashed in the lamp light and turned my hand to stone.

The long nights were upon us and a part of me were glad not to be living in a cave and worrying all the time whether I'd freeze or starve to death first. Nevertheless I sat at my window for hours, looking toward my mountain and thinking of my bear.

Cook came calling.

'You got Fox to thank for getting you out of that mess,' she said. 'I know, I know, it weren't fair what you were accused of, but to my mind you were lucky to get a suspended sentence and that in spite of Rain's influence. There int nothing but grief and loss up that mountain, my girl,' she went on. 'Best to make your life here, where you're safe.'

'But what about my bear?'

Cook shook her head sadly. 'She's a wild animal, Snow. She can't live in the city and you can't live in the forest. You got to make your peace with that.'

My face showed I were far from peaceful and she tried to cheer me up. 'You got your coming of age to look forward to. I hear there's a party in the planning.'

It were Fox's plan for us to be wed as soon as it could be arranged. And for him, in this town, that weren't a problem. He'd planned a dance for my coming of age and, anticipating I'd agree to his proposal, to celebrate our engagement with his peers.

Dressmakers came to the house and measured me for new clothing. I were made a gown just like the one I'd never worn, the one that had been painted instead of my real clothing in the picture on plates and posters at the market. It was pretty, I can't say it weren't. And it fitted me just like it should.

On the night of the dance I braided my hair like I always wore it, hanging over one shoulder. It were grown back now, not as long but reaching part-way down my back. I was looking for a way to feel like myself. My fingers itched to run through my bear's scruff and my legs felt twitchy. I needed to walk. I'd be glad even to be wading through snow to my thighs with frozen feet if I could feel I were living in my own skin again.

My knife sat atop a dresser, polished now, its strange writing showing clear on the bone handle, the blade sharpened by one of Fox's people. My furs were folded away in a drawer and I opened it now to run my hands over them.

There were a gathering formed at the gate to see us in our finery, and I were being called. At the last second, walking out the door, I went back to the dresser and lifted the she-bear fur, settling it around my shoulders. There, I thought. That's something.

Fox frowned a little when he saw but took my arm and we walked to the gate. There were dark clouds piling up to the south. Not being outside in it, these days I always felt two steps behind changes in the weather. Having four walls and a roof over my head was making me complacent.

Just like Little Bear, I raised my chin and sniffed the air. It were bitter cold and those clouds told me it were very bad weather. Maybe an ice-storm.

Standing in front of the gathered crowd, I put aside my weather forecasting and tried to smile. They weren't wishing us anything but good, and all friendly faces and calling out congratulations and happy birthday to me. Even the children were looking at me shyly and I bent to take some of the posies they offered. It seemed that accepting Fox's offer had redeemed me in the eyes of the city people. Some held up pictures already showing me wearing a wedding dress.

I left the speaking to Fox. It were what he did for a living, after all. I was getting to know the life of a politician now. How it worked. He told the people that I were looking forward to serving my suspended sentence under his roof and grateful for the mercy of the court. Although, he said, there were more to the story than were told in court and this would come to light in the fullness of time.

Glancing out over the crowd a particular figure caught my gaze. I shifted to my tiptoes to get a clearer view and our eyes met, just for a second. There were no mistaking his height and bearing. I'd pick it anywhere, through a blizzard if I had to. The hunter, hooded, was standing at the back, watching and listening. And the meeting of our eyes were all it took to remember all that I needed to.

I'd sent him away but here he was. Had he forgiven my harsh words in Cook's kitchen? The whispered conversation I'd overheard in Noelly's dairy came back to me. That our betrothal was none but a joke to him. Maybe it had been to him, but it were no joke to me when offering myself were all that I had. The mind being always a few steps behind the heart perhaps it knew then what I were only just coming to know now.

The ring resting near my knuckle burned.

Fox joined me in the fancy front room when he were done talking to his gathering.

'I can't be wed to you,' I told him.

'Snow,' he said, coming over and taking hold of my shoulders. I shrugged him off.

'If you need some time for us to get more acquainted, I don't object to that. It's just the sooner we're wed, the sooner you're free of your stepmother. She won't have any say over you once I'm your husband.'

'Why, because then you'll be the one to have say over me?'

He started to object but I spoke up again. 'I can't marry you because I'm promised to another. I were a child, that's true, but even so, I can't forget it. It were a trade for my life and it hasn't been settled.'

Fox's eyes, which were usually soft and kind when he were looking at me, seemed to harden. His lips pressed together.

'You owe me a debt too, Snow. It isn't gentleman-like to remind you, but the bail alone is more than you can repay in your lifetime, and living here with me is a condition of your freedom.'

I thought back to when Fox had slipped a ring on my finger. I'd been so relieved not to be going to gaol that I'd agreed to his proposal without thinking on what it really meant.

First of all, years of house arrest, shut up like I hated being, and then, even if I were let out one day, living in a city. At first the crowds and markets and lamplit evenings were a novelty and pleased me, but now, with the prospect of spending the rest of my days here, I could just about hear the mountain calling to me, pulling me back like it owned me. Even exile in the deep south were beginning to look better than staying in the city.

It weren't to do with Fox. He had helped me without my asking for it, out of what appeared to be kindness. But I was starting to see how much having me at his side increased his popularity. I were famous in my own right. Not for being or doing anything that I could see, but because I seemed like the idea of something to city folk. Maybe that idea was the freedom that they couldn't have, shut away behind the walls of the city. But any sensible person could see that it were a harsh life in the open and that not many could survive it. Safer behind the wall and in the company of other people in lean times.

I knew that mountain life was cruel, having died myself on more than one occasion, and only been saved by luck. City folk liked the idea of me and my bear, not to live our life themselves, but for their imaginations. It's what Rain had exploited, and Fox were doing the same thing. Instead of trying to kill me like my stepmother, he was just trying to keep me.

'The problem being, this int my idea of freedom, Fox. I'd rather be exiled in the deep south than confined by walls. Any walls, even fancy ones.'

Fox turned his back on me, gazing into the fire, one hand resting on the mantelpiece.

'Please try to understand,' I said. 'I've spent most of my life shut away for one reason or another. Either that or I been running. I came here to try to clear the way to a different kind of living. But it weren't to be.'

Still not looking at me, Fox spoke softly. 'If it's the hunter you mean to keep your word to then you should know that he never had any intention of keeping his. He came back to the city to clear his own name, not to help you. He's on the run too, did you know that?'

Fox turned to me, eyes hard. He were a man used to getting what he wanted, I saw that now.

'Your hunter is wanted for murder. He agreed to bring you in in exchange for the charges against him being dropped. You made your choice, Snow. You have a new vow to keep.'

He went away then and left me alone. Soon after I was sent upstairs to be out of the way of the party preparations. I paced my room and turned over my thoughts. I knew the hunter had done bad things, starting with leaving me in the forest, just a child, and since then how he'd lived showed in the lines in his face and the pain in his eyes. And if he'd brought me back to the city for his own benefit, I had to admit that made sense. He'd been sneaking around day and night at Cook's place, being as cold to me as he'd ever been. Like he was trying to push me away.

It were possible he'd been making the arrangements to turn me over to my stepmother.

But then he hadn't.

And adding up against that, he'd twice saved my life. First by putting a hole in the she-bear, then by bringing me back from dead. And in between he'd had to make a living as best he could, same as everyone. He were a hunter and that meant killing. If that's the way you live your life, then what's the difference between one life and another? I weren't in a position to judge the hunter on what he'd killed.

And besides, if my weeks in the city had shown me anything, it were that accusations by city people were as likely to be false as true.

The party

》————→

Looking for a place to think where no one could find me, I was drawn by a room down the hall a ways from mine. With everyone in a bustle downstairs, I let myself in, closing the door with a soft click.

The walls were lined with shelves of books, more'n I'd ever seen together in one place, which weren't saying all that much if I'm truthful. I ran my fingers along the spines. It would be something good about living in this house to have all these books to myself. I could start on one shelf and read my way along til I hit the end. It weren't like having a body free in the forest, but a mind is always free to roam where it likes.

I pulled back the curtains a crack to let in some light over a table strewn with papers. I guessed they'd been left out without fear of my reading them for Fox still thought me illiterate. So it were a small triumph to stand and look over his private business.

A model sat in one corner and I realised with a gasp it was a perfect recreation of my mountain.

I pored over it, fascinated. Some of the river runs were not quite right, and likewise the passes were a little wayward, but all in all it were the same map I carried in my head. Except at the base of the mountain, set near the river, was a settlement that I knew weren't there. I puzzled over it. Tiny houses built from clay were lined up along streets running off a square, all behind a thick high wall, just like the city I stood in now. The model was so detailed even tiny people walked the streets. Labels showed where the market would be and it seemed different quarters of the city had been set aside for different groups, one called Voyagers.

I rifled through some papers, my eye skimming over the words. Picking up one set, placing them down, going to another. Lots were lists of calculations that I couldn't make out, but there was also correspondence going back and forth.

It dint take long, not even for a mountain girl, to figure it out.

Back in my room I had a view over the city and the weather coming in. It weren't a night to be out in but when darkness fell that dint stop the carts pulling up in front of the house and fancy people hopping out, clutching coats about them, being whipped by the rising winds. I watched them lit up by the lamps lining the drive.

The women wore dresses in linen of all colours, decorated with feathers and furs. Gems and precious metals strung around throats and hung from earlobes caught the light and gleamed. As the guests arrived I heard voices carrying up the stairs from the grand ballroom and then the band started to play. I ran my fingers over the blade of my knife, polished like new, before stowing it with my furs safely in my pack.

Then I dressed for a party.

I wore the dress of blood red with the bodice of blue,

embroidered with white flowers. To feel like myself, though, I took a cool coal from the fire and, peering into a mirror, marked my brow like a falcon. The long charcoal lines gave me a fierce glare that suited my mood. Then I tied my silk scarf around my hair and, holding my head high, left my room and descended the stairs. The room was lit by glittering spirit lamps, putting a glow on the faces of the people speaking to one another in small groups.

I drew their attention by taking the stairs slow, and one by one the faces turned to look at me. I stopped near the bottom and smiled. Applause broke out and guests called my name, but it seemed to me there were two sides to all the faces looking back at me. Behind their eyes they were thinking something different to what showed on the outside. There were certainly some in the room who knew about Fox's plans, and had their signatures on the papers upstairs.

Once I was old enough and we were wed, Fox would claim the mountain in my name. He planned to become mayor and relocate the city. I'd seen him at work. He was an excellent politician, and he'd gathered his support carefully and thoroughly. I could see that by looking around the room before me.

It were supposedly my party, but nothing that happened here tonight would be in my interest.

When Fox saw me, he stepped up, taking my hand. To read his face it were like the afternoon's discussion had never happened. I were taken around the room on his arm, meeting people I weren't likely to see again but nevertheless playing my part as Fox wanted. I smiled and nodded as the guests congratulated me one by one. I received their well wishes with thanks and that was all that were required of me.

So much for the social skills the hunter were always telling me I lacked. I had no need of them after all.

When we'd passed around the room I told Fox I wanted to dance. My feet were itching to move in the slippers I'd been given. Fox was a good dancer and was more than happy to draw the eyes of the gathering to him and his captured mountain girl.

The band were the same players we'd danced to in the lowlands bar when Fox and I first met. It seemed a coincidence til I caught the eye of the singer and felt she saw right through me. Dark of eye and skin, dressed in a floral dress with frills at the hems and large golden hoops hanging from her ears, she clapped her hands to each side and stamped her heel to the wooden floor in time with the strings.

Once I was dancing, I forgot my troubles. There was nothing could worry me while my feet flew, barely touching the floor, partnered with Fox. The horns of the band filled my ears and I closed my eyes for the feeling of flying. My skirt swirled around me like water over river pebbles and I felt at one with the movement and the music. Life pumped back into my veins. It was almost as good as being out in the forest with my bear.

I had to keep my wits though, for it were a part of my plan to be the centre of attention and then disappear from plain sight.

As the party went on, most everyone in the room was drawn onto the dance floor, the bar drunk dry and forgotten, the band dripping with sweat. They were playing a song that had been building in speed and volume, sweeping the dancers into a whirling throng. When it seemed the band couldn't play any faster, their fingers flying over keys and strings, the singer lifted her arms and brought them down, the lamps in the room seeming to dim, and the music stopped, the last notes dying away. There was a moment of hush before the drummer began a slow beat on his instrument that gradually gathered speed. When the melody came in the singer raised her arms bringing in the horns and strings in a rhythm that captured its audience and the crowd burst into dance once again.

That was when the singer looked to me and pointed to the door. How she guessed my plan, I have no idea.

Passing quickly through the darkened kitchen, I let myself out and retrieved my pack from under the window where I'd thrown it from my room. There weren't time to change out of my gown but I slipped on trousers and boots and, on top, all the layers I had. The wind were as high as it gets behind the city walls and ice starting to fall from the sky when I walked out through Fox's front gates, left open for guests, and strode through the deserted streets of the city.

The funeral

You must have cut a lonely figure walking away from your own birthday party that evening, Little Queen. I weren't watching over you then, it being more than my heart could bear to see you dancing with Fox again. If I'd known then what were coming – well, there int anything I can change now. You were following your path, Snow, and I know now what I didn't know then, that it's my path to follow yours.

Stoat must have been watching the house and set off through the streets after you. The storm dint stop you, or even slow you down, if I'm guessing right. Once it were in your head to go back to the mountain, not even an ice-storm blowing in from the deep south could have changed your mind.

He waited til you'd passed through the city gates, deserted at that time of night, in that weather, so no one to see you leaving. After that he dint wait long. The frozen rain was blowen in sideways by then, maken it hard to walk upright. Maybe he were chilled through and wanted to get back to a warm fire and a brew. Or he might have just seen his chance. It were a short way out of the city and maybe you paused at the crossroads, wondering which way to find your bear. It was that hesitation he took advantage of. Having missed you once, he weren't going to let another one go wide. He lined up his shot, this time with the wind behind him, and let loose his crossbow. The bolt flew strong and true and you fell where you stood. Right there on those crossroads. He must have pulled his arrow free and taken it with him, but it were no mystery to me who was responsible for killing you a second time.

It was bright morning the next day before a wagoner hauling a load of grain came across you. There weren't nothing living about you, but he saw who you were and laid you on the back of his cart, among the bags. He called out as he came through the city gates with his sad cargo. He called out that he carried the Little Queen, shot dead through the chest. In the quiet of the morning, his voice rang through the streets and people came out of their houses. Seeing you there for themselves they cried out and some followed along behind. By the time the wagoner reached the council, most of the city were following along or there to meet him.

You were laid out in a glass case in the great chamber. Your head on a silk pillow and your hair spilled out across it. The women dressed you in clothes I never seen you in, a black dress covered in flowers and lace at the breast to hide your wound. When I came to see you I had the she-bear fur and the ratty old dog I gave you in the forest those long years ago when I left you there. How I could've done that, I can't think now. You were just a child and I thought I were generous gifting you a skin as your only protection against the cold. I covered you in your coffin with those furs. They did all they could to protect you in life and so they might as well go with you wherever you were bound to next.

I went out to the so-called sanctuary and cut through the wire to let your bear out. You'd been told it were open fields and rehabilitation but I saw for myself the hoops and balls left about that told the animals were being trained for travelling fairs. Little Bear seemed to know what I was about the way she does, and me being next best to you, followed me back to the city like the faithful creature she is. Once the coffin were set in place in the chamber they let her in to see. After that she were inconsolable. She lay down on the cold tile floor and wouldn't stir to eat nor drink, no matter how I enticed her with her favourite sweet meats.

It weren't surprising to see such behaviour from your bear. It were plain to all she was devoted to you in life and now in death too. But what was surprising were all the birds come to see you. They swooped in through the doors and windows of the grand chamber left open and gathered in the rafters, uncommon quiet and solemn. Those green mountain parrots came in numbers never before seen in the lowlands. And there were hawks and bellbirds and kingfishers and honeyeaters and tomtits and even city pigeons. Usually too dim to do much except pick at crumbs, they lifted their feet in their odd waddle and walked right through the doors, like they were entitled to it.

Once there the birds showed no sign of leaving. Just sitten up there in the roof beams and all around the chamber on any available perch, quiet and still. The falcon, supposed to be trained to come to me only, were like the conductor of this strange bird choir. Leaving me, she took up a perch at your feet and there were no persuading her away. She sat with her head bowed, and it were completely mad to think it, but she gave the impression of a priestess in prayer.

I never seen anything like it in my life. And that's sayen something after my time walking the mountain with you.

Fox invited the people to come and pay their last respects. It weren't long before a queue formed that stretched all the way to the city wall. They came quiet and sad, dropping flowers first around you, and then around your coffin, then on the floor and after that they got so deep that people coming in later had to wade through a sea of posies up to their thighs.

Even the miners came. Little Bear raised her lips to snarl at them, and they filed around your coffin, steppen carefully by her. The same men who'd kept you as good as a slave, assaulted you, and then chained your bear and tried to sell you, now mourning your death.

I stood close and I heard them muttering their sorries. Some of them more shamefaced than others. Once they'd paid their respects they set up a guard of honour on the steps of the great chamber. Standing as straight as they could given their profession, picks and shovels held beside them.

I kept watch. I sat in the shadows and no one noticed me, all of them having eyes only for you lying there, quiet and still as stone. Sometimes a child, holding onto her mother's hand, would look toward me and catch my eye. I must have looked a fright, for that was what I saw on their faces. They saw me and moved nearer their mothers, hiding their faces from the grief they saw on mine.

If only I'd stayed close, Little Queen. If only I'd stayed close.

The day came when the last mourner filed through the door and waded through the sea of flowers to look upon your face. It were the singer from the band you loved so much. She were dressed all in black, even her lips stained with ink, her ears hung about with golden loops and a lace veil covering her hair. With her dark eyes and skin, she looked like your kin, Little Queen. She lingered at your side, whispering words quietly that I couldn't quite catch. I looked at her sharply and she met my gaze.

'I had a part in this,' she told me. 'I helped her leave. But worry not, Hunter, for this death will not be her last.'

And then she left.

When Fox closed the great chamber doors he left without so much as a glance to you. He'd forgotten me, sitting as I was in the shadows. It were after he left, and as the last of the light was fading from the day, that my falcon lifted her head and cried out like I'd never heard before. And with her call, all the birds in the rafters set up their own mournful evening song. And though it were an unholy mix of cries, it seemed to blend together into a sweet and sad funeral hymn, not a dirge like you'd expect at such a time, but instead like they were trying to lift the roof with their devotion.

I made my way across the floor as well as I could and stood over you to say goodbye. I'd not be staying for the funeral. The way Fox had it planned, it weren't nothing you would have wanted. There were already banners flying and processions rehearsing in the streets. I couldn't stand to see your death made into a spectacle. Instead I aimed to try and convince Little Bear to follow me back to the mountain where we both belonged.

Approaching your glass coffin, I laid my filthy hand lightly on your brow. I thought of the time I'd found you frozen in the snow, when you looked exactly the same. Face so still and the black of your eyelashes resting on your cheeks like feathers. It weren't my place and I had no right but it were the last time I'd see you and I couldn't leave without placing my lips on yours.

Our lips had never met in all the time of our betrothal and I were full of regret that I'd waited til now. I pressed my mouth to yours and let my tears fall freely to your cheeks, making tracks on your skin. I were surprised to feel something like warmth, but thought it must have been my fancy. With the shaft going straight through your chest like it did, there were no surviving such a wound. You were dead and it was as much my fault as it were the hand that let fly the bolt.

There was nothing in my life before or since that equalled the effort I made to pull my lips away from yours. The bird choir sang around me, filling the chamber with sound and, I imagined, perhaps even passing through the clouding over to reach the heavens of old.

I dragged myself out of the chamber, swinging the doors wide, letting out the sound of the bird choir. To my astonishment I saw that a quiet crowd had gathered in the square. They knelt on the paving and held their hands together in vigil. Candles were lit all around that lent a soft yellow glow to the faces of men, women and children. When I appeared at the top of the steps, they looked up from their contemplations but, seeing it were me, paid me no more notice. I were stunned at the size of the crowd, all those who had been moved by the injustice that had befallen you.

The last of the dusk light faded. With it, the bird choir hushed.

And then a gasp arose from the gathering of people and small cries of wonder went up.

I turned and there you were, Snow. Standing in your black

funeral finery, a flush returned to your cheeks, bare feet already freezing on the cold stone of the council's grand steps.

You stood with a hand pressed to your wound which was oozing bright-red blood through your fingers, your face a picture of confusion.

I was at your side in a few short steps, catching hold as the shock of the cold night set your legs buckling. The crowd was rippling with excitement, people climbing up from their knees and crying out with joy at seeing you standing before them alive instead a dead.

Little Bear came to your side, and now it seemed like she'd known all along. Her laying immovable at your feet weren't despair but instead a patient vigil.

And then, following Little Bear through the doors, came a great swooping of the bird choir, making a new formation spiralling up into the night sky. The crowd turned their faces to watch in wonder and at that moment, the clouding over parted.

Some fell to their knees again, this time in awe, many having lived their whole lives under the clouds, never seeing the stars. The deep blue-black of the universe were revealed to them and just as it should, it struck them mute. It were mid-winter and the clouds slowly drifted apart, the night sky showing itself for the first time in many long seasons. And above, as if put there for you, hung the star ship under sail.

The mountain

>>--------→

The hunter and I sat in our forest camp, half a day's walk from the chateau. We'd left the city behind, anxious to get back to the mountain, walking up through fields of tussock grass, washed clean by rain and dried by a sun shining clear out of a blue sky. My wound were healing clean, and my legs worked fine.

The doctor who examined me after I'd risen from my coffin said it were a miracle the bolt missed every artery and organ. And lying still through the icy night as I had chilled me to the bone and stopped the bleeding. Not for the first time, I'd warmed up slow and come back to life.

To me it were the least surprising part about my weeks in the city but the people were overcome with the marvel of it and the coincidence of the clouding over parting at the same time I rose from the dead. They held me responsible for the reappearance of the stars and the moon.

I dint do anything, I kept saying over and over, but it were hopeless. They were convinced and there was nothing I could say to tell them otherwise.

I been dead before and could be I'll die again in the mountain cold before I leave this life for good. After the clouding over cleared, the hunter and I stayed with Cook while my wound were tended to and healed some. It were a faster recovery in the warmth of Cook's kitchen than I'd had up in the cave in the mountains. And if I were feverish it was with longing to get back to my forests. As soon as I could place one foot in front of the other, the hunter and I bade Cook goodbye again, tearful this time.

Once beyond the city, Little Bear made us laugh by galloping through the grassy fields in the sunshine that was still a wonder.

'Maybe we can't be calling her Little anymore, Snow,' the hunter said. 'Look at that roundness there in her middle. She needs a long walk and we'd better be getting started on it.'

Sitting around a low fire in a camp with the hunter brought quiet down on my shoulders like a warm fur. But the hunter weren't feeling the same contentment. He had a tightness in the corners of his mouth and his gaze was restless.

'Did you take me to the city thinking you'd hand me over for the reward?' I asked him. I needed to know.

'No. I never thought I'd hand you over. But knowing where you were was the only hand I had to play. Remember I told you about your stepmother getting it in her head that the Voyagers had brought a sickness with them that terrible long nights season?'

I nodded. I did remember. 'When she evicted them you took pity and guided them down the mountain.'

The hunter bowed his head.

'Another group come to the gate soon after. They had travelled long and hard by sea and then over the passes, trying to make it before the end of the long days, but weather descended on them while they were still up high and they lost a lot of people to the cold. They were desperate for shelter by the time they reached our gate. And it was bad luck Rain had so recently turned hard of heart toward Voyagers.

'I never saw such suffering in people before. The men were barely standing, the women faring little better, but all the same still holden babies on their hips or bound with rags across their backs. They were half-frozen and starving. There was no more walking in them. It weren't like the ones I'd taken down the mountain. That lot were in good health after staying with us for a time, or as near as they'd been in a while, anyway.

'Your stepmother came down and took one look at this new group and forbade anyone opening the gate. She said they were infested with disease and likely to die before long anyways. We'd only be drawing it out if we took them in. We hardly got enough for ourselves, she told people, ifen we share with every passing stranger we won't make it through. And besides, did we want to die of whatever disease these Voyagers were carrying? Hadn't we already lost enough of our own children?

'I dint believe for a second she were worried about more people dying. She was only worried about having enough for herself. I argued as best I could, and so did Cook. We said we'd give up our own beds. And I said I'd go and hunt, whatever the conditions. But even to Rain it was clear there was very bad weather setting in and she told me I weren't going anywhere while that kept up. She told me if I opened the gates I'd be walking out through them and never coming back.

'The Voyagers dint understand our language, but they understood clear enough they weren't being let in. The men turned, holding onto their dignity, and the women's faces turned to stone. It were only the children who let their feelings show. One small girl, standing in the snow bundled in all the layers her folks had to give her, looked into my face and I couldn't bear to look back into hers. She were no bigger than you when I left you in the forest that day. A memory that dint make me feel none better at the time. I pointed them to the forest, thinking it would give them some cover if they could make it there.

'It were a deadly storm that came down on us then. The wind ripped roofs off the chateau and froze our animals where they stood. It raged for near on a week. And then it were quiet. All of a sudden liken. You know how that happens, sometimes? You're near deaf from the racket and then the silence falls and seems almost as loud.

'As soon as I could, I went out looking for the Voyagers and it dint take long to find them. It's a scene I can't ever shake from my memory, no matter how hard I try. And sometimes it comes up and grabs me by the throat. Then I can't hardly breathe and it's like I'm standing there all over again.

'Frozen solid all of them, lying about in the snow. But worst of all, the little girl. She died with her eyes wide open, still looking into my face and seeing nothing there that would save her.

'Word got back to the city about the death of a group of people seeking refuge and eventually the council sent someone to see. Refusing them hospitality were a crime that weren't going to go unpunished and your stepmother saw it straight away. She told the officer it were me who'd turned them away. That I was her hunter and in charge of the chateau's security. That it were my judgement that the Voyagers were diseased and we couldn't take them in without risking the lives of everyone. She said it made her heartsick to turn them away and she'd cried and got on her knees to beg me to open the gate.

'I were arrested, to be taken to the city to stand trial. I dint raise any objections to Rain's lies because in my heart I knew that I was as guilty as she were. It was in my power to let those people in. I dint have to listen to Rain. I could have locked her in her room. But I didn't, so it were as much my fault as hers they all died. I deserved to be punished as much as anyone. I were tired and heartsick about being the cause of such misery. What kind of a man am I that leaves girls in the snow to die?

'It were Cook who came and convinced me that there were still some good I could do. She were sure you lived and that it were in my power to protect you from Rain. And it weren't any trouble for me to slip away, especially when Cook unlocked the door and passed me my firearm and furs, the council officer passed out drunk on her needle beer and neglecting his guarding duties. As I left she told me the world, however disordered it be, does have good people in it, and I should run now and stay away.

'I hugged her tight then, it being a wonder she'd kept her kind heart all those years in spite of the testing she'd been put through. She always said she stayed to keep on feeding her people and doing what she could to put matters right that had been put wrong by your stepmother. Someone had to, she said.

'So when we got to the city I proposed an arrangement with Rain. I would face justice for my part in the Voyagers' deaths in return for her setting you free. But she wouldn't hear it.

Instead she said she'd pardon me in exchange for you. Some cheek offering me a pardon for her crime.'

Leaving the city behind weren't hard for me or the hunter. It didn't take long for Fox's men to arrest Stoat, and with me as witness to my own murder, and others from the chateau to verify the Hunter's version of how the Voyagers died, Rain were found guilty on all counts by the same panel of judges that heard my trial. This time the outcome was more to my liking.

The hunter and I were pardoned. With Rain convicted, she was no longer entitled to hold land and guardianship of the chateau and the mountain it stood on finally reverted to me. She spent some time in a stone cell but without her power or her people she were a sad creature.

My conscience pulled at me, leaving her shut up, knowing as I did what that were like, even though she'd brought it on herself, and more. But she'd loved my father, of that I were sure. And if looking after him while he died slow and painful were all the good she'd done in her life then it was a mercy to let her live the rest of her days in company with none but her own still small voice.

I made Fox grant a suspension of her sentence and she went to stay with Cook, who opened her kind heart once again.

It were there in Cook's kitchen she sat when I last saw her, my arm strapped across the wound in my chest. She wore plain clothes and worked at cutting onions in the worst way, slow and dull soas to make you weep. She set the knife down when she saw me.

'Rain,' I said, 'you must tell me of the riders who came to

the chateau on the dark night before you sent me to the forest with the hunter. What did they ask of you?'

My stepmother wiped her eyes on a cloth and sniffed. 'They were looking for a Voyager girl. I asked them, how were I to tell a particular one? There were so many and all looking wretched. They said this one were carrying a child though only a child herself. And that it were many seasons ago. Then I suspected they were looking for your mother, the one who birthed you and died in the doing as your father had told it to me. I said that girl and the baby were long dead before my time. They dint seem to be honest men. The opposite. They were wild of eye, and rough, not from around here. I thought it for your own good they dint hear about you.'

'Yes, best you order my heart cut from my chest yourself,' I said.

Rain pursed her lips and turned her face away. 'That's all I know, Snow. Leave me be now.'

I sold the land at the base of my mountain to the council soas they could move the city inland. It were the only sensible plan, in that I was in agreement with Fox. There would be a whole quarter set aside for Voyagers seeking refuge. There would also be a permanent base at the high pass to meet travellers and ensure safe passage to the new city. I carried in my pack the title to the mountain chateau, now in my name, plus the money I'd made on the sale of the lowlands. There was more than enough to repair all the roofs and stock the cellars for the long nights that were still coming.

The sky above our camp was clear and the wonder of the moon hanging like a spirit lamp in the heavens meant there was no true darkness in the forest anymore. The snow gleamed and I could even make out the needles on the whispering branches over our heads. The trees were pleased to see us and pulled their limbs in close. During the dark hours, birds that had never seen the moon before called to one another, confused about whether it were night or day.

No one expected the cloud cover to stay away for good, but the blue sky were a marvel no one could leave alone for long, people all over the island pausing in their work and gazing into the vastness, checking it were still there, and drinking it in while it lasted.

My wound ached at the end of the day and I still wore my arm bound across my chest. Now and again my mind unbidden went back to the moment I was shot. The memory rose up in front of me and made my heart race, even though it were long over with.

I was walking away from the party, my dress getting in a tangle around my ankles every few steps, I'd paused at the crossroads to get it free and find my bearings. I weren't exactly sure which was the way to the sanctuary where my bear were being held. I guessed it be to the east, and just as I turned that way I felt a kick in the back, as if from a horse, but there being none close, I were puzzled. My legs folded under me and I found myself looking up to a sky of racing cloud. I was distracted a moment by the cold wonder and fury of it before my vision were blurred by pain. It bloomed from my back and spread from there til I could no longer tell where it started or ended. Just then a dark figure loomed over me, blocking out the sky.

'I'll have that back soas I don't get chased down and pelted with pebbles for being the one put a bolt through the precious Little Queen.'

Stoat, still working for my stepmother, reached down and I saw he'd put an arrow clean through me. He clasped the shaft, placed a boot on my shoulder as brace, and pulled. The pain of the bolt moving through my flesh from back to front were the last thing I knew. Black closed in and I must have passed out.

I pushed away the memory and went around the fire to sit close to the hunter for comfort. In spite of the beauty of the sparkling cold clear night, he sat with his head hung between his knees.

I took his hand with my good one and waited for him to tell me what were on his mind.

'You called me monster once and you were right. All I've ever been is a hunter, but I never took any pleasure in killen. I always tried to do it quick and clean and always to fill people's bellies. I've kilt to protect those I love as well, when I had to,' he added, pulling his hand from mine. 'But those Voyagers, I had a hand in killen them. I did. And that makes me a monster as much her. I had to make it right again, Snow. Somehow.

'The meeting between me and the man you took for a miner were to try get word back to those Voyagers' families who died while I stood my watch. I wrote an account and spoke to an agent who transports goods around the island, and sometimes the rest of the world. It was to have been sent back the way those people had come from.

'I described them as best I could remember. How many men, how many women, children and their ages, anything else I could think of in the manner of distinguishing features.

'But, Snow, it's a one-way journey. No one who finishes here turns around and goes back again. All the winds and currents flow the wrong way. And letters, like birds, can't fly backwards over mountains and oceans.

'What you saw from Cook's rooftop that night was the agent giving me back my letter, having found no way to send it. It burns now in my pocket. But I'll carry it with me so long as I can put one foot in front of the other, to remind me never to let my heart turn cold. I'm finished with leaving children in the snow. I were just lucky when I left you, Little Queen. You being you, and having the touch with the forest and the birds, whatever gift it is that you have, it saved you. But that were no thanks to me. I been sorry ever since, and I'll be sorry ever more.'

I understood then how the extra cares had come to be written in the lines of the hunter's face. They were drawn there by his part in Rain's crimes. By following her orders he were complicit in them. There were no getting around that. My stepmother were a bully, that much was true. But a bully can only get her way when others do her bidding.

'When I called you a monster I dint know what I were sayen,' I told him. 'You saved me from my stepmother, from the she-bear, and dying of cold twice. That's four lives you saved, no matter they all happen to be mine. How many died in the snow? Were it eight? Nine? Then that's how many more lives you got yet to save. And the rest of your life to do it.'

When he looked up at me again, there was hope in his dark eyes.

'Also, I think there may be some who know how to get back to those islands. And we'll do what we can to find them. You and me.'

I ran my fingers over the lines in his face. I told him that I was sorry for those Voyagers and I was sorry for his suffering.

And I told him we were no longer betrothed. We were wed.

The Successful Release of an Apex Predator: A survey of the new endemic fauna of South and North Zealand

————≪

Professor James T. Longfort, *Post-Nature*, vol. 2, 2072

In the immediate aftermath of the global sea level rises of the late 2030s, many of the species kept in captivity in the former nation of New Zealand were released into the wild. Many did not survive, but some did, migrating and establishing populations throughout the mainland (the larger of the two islands, now known as 'South'). This article provides a summary of the events surrounding the release of new species and how those have prospered.

After the end of the modern climate era, generally agreed to have dated from the last ice age 7000 years ago to the beginning of the Anthropocene (now officially dated from the catastrophic collapse of west Antarctica that took place in the Southern Hemisphere summer of 2035), there has been a complete change in the fauna inhabiting the islands of North and South Zealand. After the subsequent three-metre rise in sea levels over the ensuing decade, the two islands that sit in the lower south corner of the Pacific Ocean were significantly inundated but the small human communities of the islands were able to adapt more nimbly than many larger, more unwieldy populations elsewhere in the world. However, with the collapse of the fossil fuel industry and the worldwide ban on freight shipping and air travel, the flooded islands, along with many nation-states in similar geographical circumstances, were cut off from the global economy. After the immediate crisis had passed and most of the population had relocated to inland cities, the central government (while it remained so before following the rest of the planet into decentralised, local governing bodies) dropped 'New' from the nation's name to reflect the vastly altered state of the nation's geography and politics.

Over subsequent generations, the human birthrate plunged, as it did on other continents. Fewer resources and much harsher weather patterns drove an increase in infant mortality and reduced life expectancy. Vaccination levels plummeted when the supply of pharmaceuticals was interrupted and then became unreliable. However, as inhabitants adapted to the change in environment, and populations (and therefore disease transmission) became more static, the numbers of humans stabilised. The milestone birthrate of 2.0 was eventually reached in the early 2060s but infant mortality remained high. Many women living in remote locations did and still do not have access to specialist prenatal care resulting in a return to pre-modern-era maternal death rates during childbirth.

In the post-global era, with human populations travelling far less widely than in previous generations, with decentralised systems of government (similar to the local councils of the modern era), there is less pollution entering the environment and almost no industrial-scale production. However, the challenges presented by planet-wide permanent stratus cover (referred to colloquially as 'clouding over' and discussed in more detail in J.L. Anderson's landmark paper 'Permanent Stratus Cover: Cascading causes in the post-global era', Post-Climate Journal, vol. 3, 2057) and its climatic impact on the islands of Zealand have been significant. The four-season annual cycle present in the higher latitudes gradually changed to the two-season pattern that used to be found only in equatorial and polar zones. In the Southern Hemisphere this manifests as one season of short days, the other of long days. However, under thick stratus cover, the long days are bookended with long twilight periods at dawn and dusk where the diffused sun is weak. Increased snowfalls, even commonly to sea level across the mainland, along with ice-storms that roll in regularly from the treacherous and unpredictable weather patterns in the Southern Ocean, make conditions harsh for all but the toughest of fauna, such as those that evolved through the last ice age, like Zealand bird life.

With a lower human population, the natural environment of Zealand flourished. Forests and waterways previously under threat from over-farming and pollution were no longer under the same pressure. In the emergency evacuations immediately following the west Antarctic ice-shelf collapse and subsequent ocean inundation, many species were released from captivity in facilities in coastal areas, among them bears and wild dogs. Over time these apex predators assumed the role seen in some Northern Hemisphere locations, reducing the numbers of smaller, introduced rodents that had decimated the endemic bird species of the old New Zealand ecosystem. With these small predators, such as rats and stoats, now controlled by the larger bears and dogs, bird numbers soared, so to speak.

The scientific community has been aware for decades that the introduction of non-native species can have disastrous effects. The release of foxes into southern Australia by invading colonists in the early nineteenth century is one such example. The numbers of small endemic marsupial species were devastated, with many of these animals never being scientifically noted and classified before being wiped out.

The well-intentioned but disastrous release of breeding pairs of polar bears onto the Antarctic icesheet in the mid 2020s is a more recent and pertinent example. The popularity of polar bears among humans and publicity of their desperate plight in the northern polar region resulted in the approval of the Southern Polar Bear Release Scheme (SPBRS). A private company was engaged to capture, transport and release the bears onto the Antarctic ice sheet.

The bears barely survived the long pole-to-pole voyage and when finally released they failed to thrive. The exact reason for their decline remains disputed but the most popular theory is acute disorientation, an effect of reversing the magnetic poles the bear's brains had evolved to orient to. This certainly matches the observations made by scientists of the bears' behaviour on their release. In spite of being supported initially with fresh kills, the bears did not eat and instead wandered in circular patterns, as if in an attempt to find their way home.

In one of the greatest scientific misadventures of human history, the last polar bear to survive the relocation, a female dubbed Drift, was euthanised when she finally collapsed from exhaustion. The experiment was over within one southern summer, the private catch-and-release company folding amid public outrage at the unnecessary loss of life.

The release of brown bears into the Zealand landscape took place under very different circumstances. During the Inundation, with a state of emergency in place across both islands, animals kept in captivity were humanely released by their keepers to make their way inland along with the human population and survive if they could. Perhaps it was a blessing that the four African tigers and small pride of lions released from the capital's zoo sadly did not survive the flooding, while many of the great ape species voluntarily returned to captivity, almost all of their numbers soon accounted for by their keepers.

A breeding pair of brown bears, believed to be from a private sanctuary on the old South Island, survived and indeed thrived upon their release, making their way instinctively into high country. It is the progeny of one breeding pair (the sum total of brown bears listed in the DoC archives) that has resulted in the healthy population of wild bears in the South high country we see today.

It is now common to see the large parrot bird species, among them keas and kakas, living close to and among human towns and cities of Zealand. Numbers of wattle birds such as the tui have increased to what are presumed to be pre-European invasion numbers. Even the kōkako, assumed extinct in the modern era, has recovered in numbers and its distinctive call is heard throughout native forest regions of the mainland.

Most remarkable is the kakapo's recovery. The bizarre alpine parrot's habitats were saved from human encroachment and their small mammal predators' numbers vastly reduced resulting in a breeding boom. The raptor and other predator species of falcon, harrier and owl (karearea, kahu and ruru) frequent the skies. Even ocean-going mammal species such as seals, dolphins and whales have increased in numbers sufficient to allow sustainable hunting of these animals as a food source for local peoples. Councils impose strict catchments on these animals, however enforcement is ever an issue.

In conclusion, it is now accepted among scientists that the coincidental timing of a reduction in environmental pressures from human encroachment combined with the accidental release of an apex predator led first to a stabilising and second to a flourishing of the ancient endemic birdlife of the South and North islands of Zealand. However, it must be emphasised that this was not a controlled experiment undertaken by scientists but rather a rare example of an accident having a happy ending.

Acknowledgements

With heartfelt thanks to my friend Celia Jellett for her encouragement after an early reading of the manuscript, and long before that for sharing her office and her vast knowledge of children's books with me. Thanks to Corrie Hosking, who understands about everything but especially about always trying to get back to the writing. Thanks to Agata Orlowicz, my yoga sister, who read the manuscript and carried Snow in her heart from that moment. Thanks to the wonderful, intrepid Margot Lloyd for not only editing but also taking the manuscript with her all the way to New York. And to my oldest of friends Jo Case, Liz Nicholson and Michael Bollen at Wakefield, thank you. Thanks in advance to my brother Jonathon who looks after all the books; and a lifetime of gratitude to Kath and David for passing on their love of reading. Thanks lastly to my love, Ben, for never doubting I could do it, and my daughters, Asha and Mim, for not minding too much about all the writerly absent-mindedness.

Wakefield Press is an independent publishing and
distribution company based in Adelaide, South Australia.
We love good stories and publish beautiful books.
To see our full range of books, please visit our website at
www.wakefieldpress.com.au
where all titles are available for purchase.
To keep up with our latest releases, news and events,
subscribe to our monthly newsletter.

Find us!

Facebook: www.facebook.com/wakefield.press
Twitter: www.twitter.com/wakefieldpress
Instagram: www.instagram.com/wakefieldpress